A Match Made in Heaven

British Muslim women write about love and desire

Edited by Claire Chambers,
Nafhesa Ali and Richard Phillips

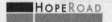

HopeRoad Publishing Ltd
PO Box 55544
Exhibition Road
London SW7 2DB

www.hoperoadpublishing.com

First published in Great Britain by HopeRoad 2020

All royalty payments from this book will go to charities working
to improve women's and girls' access to education in Pakistan.

A Match Made in Heaven and the broader research
project Storying Relationships
are supported by the Arts and Humanities Research Council (AHRC)

ISBN: 978-1-9164671-9-4
eISBN: 978-1-913109-07-3

For Jane, Asif and Tom

Contents

Introduction   ix
Claire Chambers, Nafhesa Ali and Richard Phillips

Marriage of Convenience   1
Sabyn Javeri

Ghazal   13
Nazneen Ahmed

Her Trials   26
Mariam Naeem

Boneland   39
Shaista Sadick

Tears and Tantrums   51
Sufiya Ahmed

Waiting for the Bus   67
Sairish Hussain

Contents

The Cat that Came in with the Dark   82
Sarvat Hasin

Rearranged   100
Noren Haq

Peter Pochmann Goes to Dinner   113
Bina Shah

Moments in Time   131
Sunah Ahmed

Frida's Breakfast   148
Roopa Farooki

A Simple Nature   161
Inayah Jamil

Proper and Perfect?   183
Zarina Harriri

Acid Reflux   197
Afshan D'souza-Lodhi

Love Letter   210
Shelina Janmohamed

Heartbeat   219
Ayisha Malik

Biographical Notes   237

Acknowledgements   247

Introduction

This entertaining collection of sixteen short stories about love, desire and relationships may wrongfoot some outsiders, who too often expect Muslim women to be both conservative and submissive. The reality, of course, is more complex. While some of the writers in this anthology do express a quiet piety and focus on poignant situations, others employ black humour and biting satire. Still others move fearlessly into the territory of a Muslim *Fifty Shades of Grey*.

The heroines in *A Match Made in Heaven* have the same day-to-day concerns as anyone else. For instance, one is scandalized by her would-be suitor's sloppy personal grooming, while another agonizes over the right lipstick to put on for a date. Yet another dresses up in order to make her cheating husband see how well she is doing without him – and what he is missing! Some of these women choose to wear hijabs and others do not – but the veiling issue is rarely at the forefront of their minds.

In one story, a dissatisfied wife pines for an old flame; in another, young love is tragically interrupted by the Syrian War.

Introduction

A wife struggles with her husband's move towards polygamy, while online fetishes, Islamophobia and erotica form part of the home life of a happily married couple. Themes of disability, teenage pregnancy, lesbian desire and liberated sexual behaviour at university are tackled without judgement.

A Match Made in Heaven includes work by both established and emerging authors. The latter wrote their contributions while attending workshops set up in Leeds, Bradford and Glasgow for young British Muslim women aged between sixteen and thirty. The workshops originated from a research project funded by the Arts and Humanities Research Council, entitled 'Storying Relationships'. As editors, the three of us are from diverse backgrounds, which proved an advantage as the workshops unfolded. Some participants found it easier to open up to someone from within their community, or of the same gender or sexuality, whereas others found greater freedom in speaking to individuals from 'outside'.

Given that the Qur'an makes clear that pairs (of souls) destined for each other are created in heaven, we thought our title hit the spot. It has meaning on several levels. A match, for example, may refer to a love match and a matchmaking process. It may also suggest something incendiary – a battle of wills in which harmony does not always prevail. So although our title may be read in a religious light, this is not the only possible interpretation.

Our writers are sure to challenge some received ideas about the Muslim experience. In particular, we want to unsettle the notion that young Muslims are repressed individuals who neither know what their sexual desires are, nor how to express them.

Introduction

When young Muslims write about sexual relationships, real or imagined, they may do one of two things. They may choose their words carefully, conscious of what may or may not be acceptable within their families and social circles. For that reason, in order to express themselves freely, some of our authors decided to use pseudonyms. Others have deliberately aimed their words at a society in which Muslims all too frequently find themselves misunderstood and misrepresented.

Their characters vary too: some work to 'keep it halal' while others unrepentantly explore the opposite – the 'haram'. Others still are exploring and negotiating where, if at all, the boundary between permissible and impermissible lies. Certain stories are universal in their depictions of encounters and romance, the use of digital media, infidelity, bickering and break-ups. Some stories contain more distinctively Muslim religious and cultural references, such as the semi-autobiographical narrative in which a mother gives advice to her daughter about love relationships from within a Muslim ethical framework.

A Match Made in Heaven is not alone in showcasing new writing by Muslim women about sex and relationships. Our book shares good company with a few other anthologies and a broader groundswell of assertive creativity among younger Muslim women. Yet we think our collection is a lively, unique and memorable contribution to the genre.

Most importantly, we hope you will enjoy this anthology, whoever and wherever you are. We shall now leave the stories to speak for themselves.

Claire Chambers, Nafhesa Ali and Richard Phillips

Love is the water of life.
Drink it down with heart and soul!

Rumi, Divan-i-Shams 11909

In bedrooms exhausted by desire
Someone will roll and unroll their loneliness.

Faiz Ahmed Faiz

Marriage of Convenience

Sabyn Javeri

Saira

They say matches are made in heaven. I say they are made online.

And why not? Everything else is online these days. From groceries to sex, it's all just a click away. So why should love be any different?

Funny that I never associated marriage with love before. How could I, growing up in a house where marriage was treated as a life sentence? My immigrant parents were married off young, in some obscure small town of Pakistan. Needless to say, it was an arranged marriage. They went on to spend their lives in Britain fighting each other to death but never ever contemplating divorce because marriage was, after all, a compromise that had to be struggled through for the sake of the children. So the children, in turn, had to suffer through it for the sake of their parents.

In such circumstances, how can one even begin to associate marriage with love? If anyone had asked me what marriage

1

meant, I would have said it meant suffering. But that didn't stop my pushy parents from trying to foist marriage upon me. I suspect this was more to do with realizing their own dreams of a big Asian wedding than out of any desire to see me happy. As soon as I graduated from uni and started looking for jobs, the constant nagging began: 'Get married, get married.'

I would have happily ignored them, along with the incessant chant of 'Oil your hair' and 'Learn to make curry,' but then my mother went and had a heart attack. She came out of it all right but used her illness to emotionally terrorize me. 'I want to see you a married woman before I die,' was the new weapon of choice. And so, when the time came to give in to her demands, I sought a match online. How was I to know it would actually work?

Saeed

It was about five years ago that the pressure began. I was a practising lawyer by then and the butt of all jokes at family gatherings for being the only bachelor. I had no excuse to stay unmarried since I was neither living with nor loving a white girl at the time.

Of course, this gave rise to speculation about my sexuality, which made my Pakistani parents shudder.

At the small and silent Muslim funerals in Leicester, balding uncles would slap my back and say, 'When you giving us a grandson?' They would follow this sortie with an exchange of looks and shrugs.

At over-the-top, loud Asian weddings, fat aunties would pinch my cheeks and ask, 'So, puttar, so when getting married, huh?' They'd smile broadly, showing bits of lipstick on their teeth and in shrill high-pitched tones wag their fingers at me. 'Oh, your mummy–daddy want to see your children. Why you deprive them, you bad, bad boy!' Pulling me aside, they'd close with a stage whisper, 'All the pipes are working, no?'

I'd choke and sputter, ashamed and embarrassed, but defiant and indignant too. Why should I have to change who I was?

Yet, every time my parents sat me down to tell me about a friend's son who had got married and how they couldn't wait for the day they'd see me wed, I just couldn't tell them the truth.

I. Just. Couldn't. Do. It.

Saira

Everyone was doing it. Online dating – *the halal way*. It was the latest trend amidst the newer lot of British Asians. Minder – short for Muslim Tinder, and Halal Grindr, or Hinder as we called it: these were just some of the sites that were gathering momentum when I was at uni. The only difference from mainstream apps was that here, you met with the intent to marry.

After graduation, when I settled down to a nice job and flat-share in London, the pressure to get married like a respectable Muslim girl began to drop in truckloads from the sky. So I thought, Why not – if only to shut their mouths. Maybe I could just shop around for a nice Muslim boy . . . It didn't have to end in marriage. *Did it?*

This was around the time Mum had come out of hospital. I thought if it helped with her recovery, then maybe, just maybe, I could look into this option, and if nothing else I'd make a story out of it. I'd just started writing a blog. I had discovered I loved writing, although I knew my parents would kill me if I left my boring career in corporate banking and became a full-time writer.

The first time I thought of logging on, I was clear I was doing it only to get Mum off my back. Let's face it, I was a successful young professional, financially and emotionally independent, and yet I would never be 'respectable 'or 'secure' in the eyes of my Pakistani family until I had a husband. I couldn't understand it. It made no sense. Why did I need a man to complete me? I tried making my mother understand, but when the 'Are you a lesbian?' questions began I gave up. Online matchmaking seemed a much easier option.

Saeed

I suppose I had always known. Or at least some part of me had. A part which I preferred to bury deep inside and never let surface. But just the way when you press a spring down it bounces back even harder, the more I suppressed my feelings, the stronger they became.

Don't get me wrong, I have nothing against homosexuality. It's just that I grew up in a culture where it was considered a sign of weakness. Gay. Homo. *Chakka*. The words were slurs in our culture. Swear words. Words meant to hurt you, and cause you and those who loved you pain. To be gay was to be unnatural. Un-Islamic. Haram.

I didn't have the heart to tell them I was gay. It was like a scar that plagued me, and a point came when I thought I'd rather live a lie than admit the truth to my parents. Every time they showed me a picture of a friend's daughter visiting from Pakistan, a potential match made in heaven, I knew I couldn't say yes. Still I sat through it all, constantly picking some fault or the other with the girl. Feeling bad for rejecting her, but knowing the truth would be far more painful for my parents. The closet door had shut on me. I was doomed to live my life inside it. In the dark.

Saira

'Arre, lesbian hai kya? What's this nonsense "I don't need a man shan", huh? I tell you, all this feminism—lesbianism has done your head in!' my mother would scream, making me cringe as she mixed a political ideology with a sexual identity.

What was she thinking? I often wondered as she began her rant. Did she really believe that all feminists were lesbians and all lesbians were feminists? But to point this out to her would be to bang my head against a wall. And besides, she seemed so unhappy these days. Pale and drained, yet soldiering on, my father clueless about her needs, physical *or* emotional. I had seen how my mum had lived her whole life at the mercy of Dad's moods, and to be honest it had put me off marriage for good. Yet my mum's fear, if I even mentioned I didn't want to get married, reached a pinnacle bordering on mental breakdown. 'Who will look after you in your old age?' she'd screech. 'You can't miss out on the joys of motherhood.'

Remembering the depressed childhood I'd had, with Mum blaming us as the sole reason for not being able to leave her miserable union, I wondered at her selective memory. Of course, if I were to remind her of this, she'd look at me as if I was crazy.

'Get married, get married – who will marry you once you are thirty? You'll be expired goods, motherhood doesn't wait . . .' The taunts went on daily.

One day I thought, Enough is enough. I'll get married, even if it's just to shut her up.

Saeed

Weak, weaker, weakest . . . a weakling. I'd grown up with these labels. Though I'm still not sure if the labels made me the way I am or the other way around. What I do know for sure is that I never did like being a boy. Not when I was a waif-like lad being pushed and shoved to the ground by boys who almost always seemed stronger than me, and not now that I'm a lean and strong, high-earning lawyer who can sue someone for defamation at the slightest hint of a tease.

Despite everything, the word still echoes in my head – 'Weakling'. Somewhere, somehow, I suppose I internalized it. Later on, when I began experimenting with my sex life, I realized I enjoyed being with boys. Boys who were stronger than me, who could protect me, shelter me. I told myself they completed me. They complemented my bronze skin with theirs, a shade darker or a tone lighter. They protected my slim frame with their muscular ones. They seemed right. *It* seemed right. Or so I thought . . .

Saira

I met him online. At a desi dating website. I should have known what to expect when I saw the name: *Desi Grooms & Bestest Brides*. But that's how the story goes, doesn't it? Over and over, we watch the same old formulaic Bollywood films, though we all know how romcoms end.

It was after all that nagging from my mother about still being unmarried and childless (in that order), as well as after a smattering of heartbreaks with the black boys on my course at uni, that I decided to try online dating. Trouble was, desi dating was all about getting married. You met your dates with marriage as the subtext and goal, meaning you checked each other out like sperm and egg donors. There was no romance to it: it was almost like a business transaction.

But fool that I was, I went ahead and signed up. Made a wife-material-type profile and then awaited the response. Got at least seven replies straight away. Racy Rasheed was a taxi driver in some obscure town of Pakistan, Dilwala Dilawar from the backwaters of Hyderabad was an IT professional after a visa, Big Ballz Bashir was from Bangladesh and promised to bang me senseless – I deleted him instantly. This was like Tinder for Frankenstein's bride, I thought, amused. I swiped and then swiped some more, but there wasn't a single man there who seemed sensible. Then again, how can you expect sense from a man desperate enough to search for a bride online . . . .

Saeed

Desperate times call for desperate measures. So when someone told me about desi dating I decided to give it a go. I wasn't sure why I was surprised to know that there was a Tinder for Asian weddings or a Grindr for Paki mating. Everyone was online these days, so why should desis be any different? I decided to check the site out and, dear God, it was brides galore. Brides, as in crazy OTT Asian girls who were obviously doing this out of as little interest as I was. We were all here for our parents' sake. Pretty soon I could tell who was in it for the long haul and who was just having a laugh. I decided to check out the in-it-for-a laugh people first.

And that's where I met her. Online. @SeekingSaira. She called herself a lad's lass who loved good wine, fine dining and theatre. Not your average desi bride, I thought to myself. I remember rubbing my chin and feeling the hard stubble on my cheeks as my other hand hovered over the screen. To swipe or not to swipe, that was the question.

Saira

I liked him immediately. Friendly, sensitive and game for a laugh: I couldn't help but like him. We had such a good time on our very first date. We clicked. Literally! We met again the next day and then every week, twice a week, and barely a month had passed before he proposed. I have to admit I was shocked. I wasn't expecting a whirlwind romance or lock-stock wedding, but what he told me next shocked me even more.

Saeed

Nothing was the same after that. Nothing. That is, after I met Saira. It felt as if I had reconnected with a long-lost friend. We had so much in common. Plus, she seemed as fed up with her parents as I was with mine. And she was so easy to talk to. Eventually, I told her everything. About me. And about the plan.

'MoC, they call it,' I told her. 'Short for marriage of convenience. It's an escape route for queers who can't come out to their families. And for desi girls who want a career instead of the arranged marriage and 2 point 4 children highway to heaven.'

Telling her took courage. I could have deceived her. Lots of gay men in our community do. They live their whole lives as a lie, destroying the happiness of the women they marry. And so even though at first I was afraid to broach the subject, I knew I had to come out to her. I couldn't lead her on. I told her why I wanted to marry her, and to my surprise, *she agreed*.

Saira

It took less than a week to make up my mind. He was the boy I was taking home to meet the family. Being married to him would mean I'd have space to concentrate on my career, and in time meet the person that I was meant to be with. Hopefully after I had discovered the person I was.

Or maybe, just maybe, things could change . . .

Saeed

It was a win–win situation. She had the old mother hen off her back and I made my dad breathe a sigh of relief. It was a loud one, which seemed to exhale: *Thank God he's not gay*. As if being heterosexual was the only guarantee for a safe, happy life. It made me sad to think that we had come so far yet remained so far behind. When my dad first came to Britain he worked in a factory. I was now a successful lawyer who earned in a month what he made in a year. So much had changed by way of opportunities, class and values. Yet it seemed ridiculous that they still feared my sexuality so much, refusing to accept it, hoping so much to change me.

But what really kills me is that *they weren't the only ones* . . .

Saira

We signed an MoC contract. On the face of it, it was a normal wedding, but the fine print stated that there would be no physical contact nor any sharing of financial resources. It was like our prenup, a thing alien to both our parents. For their benefit we left them out of it. 'Legal stuff,' we told them, and their eyes glazed over, for being old-world Asians, nothing scared them more than paperwork.

Saeed

When I was younger, I didn't want to be a lawyer. I wanted to be a chef. But one look at my father's face when he found me in the kitchen rolling chapatis with my mother, and I decided never to go near the stove again unless it was in the sanctity of my own kitchen among the people who knew my real self.

With Saira I could finally be myself. I loved cooking for her. Every weekend we'd have friends around, mostly mine as she seemed reluctant to tell the truth about me even to her closest associates. I'd cook for them, we'd have music, singing and an all-round good time. Evenings we'd watch telly together or decorate our little flat, which was beginning to feel more and more like home.

Sometimes my friend from work, Ben, would come around to help us. Often he'd stay the night.

Saira

In the beginning it was fine. We had a good laugh. We patted ourselves on the back for getting away with it, for having our cake and eating it too. But then things began to change. The endless meals, the barrage of visitors – always his as I couldn't really have mine mingle with his gay friends without blowing our cover. His multiple partners, his indifference to my existence, his lack of seriousness: it all began to annoy me. It was then I realized that I was falling in love with him.

Saeed

It would have worked out fine. It would have all worked out so well if only she hadn't tried to change me. In the end, even she could not accept me for the person that I am.

Saira

Love, the British Asian way: get married, fall in love, breed. But here there was no hope. He was set in his ways, and I . . . I don't know what I was thinking. I had thought I wanted companionship, freedom, choice. I wanted to date, travel, meet new people. But when the time came, I found I didn't have it in me. I wasn't the type of girl, it turned out, who could separate love from sex or sex from love. I. Just. Couldn't. Do. It. The hold of the Old Country was too great, its invisible grip around my throat taking me down. I was, in the end, no different from my mother.

Saeed

I ended it. The night she walked in on me and Ben, I held her by the arm and, half-dragging her down the hall, I ejected her from the flat. For the first time in my life, I felt powerful. No longer was I the weak boy others kicked to the ground. That night, when she wouldn't accept mine and Ben's relationship, I told her to shut up. We had gone into the bedroom but she kept knocking, begging him to stop ruining our marriage. That was the last straw.

'What marriage?' I shouted as I opened the door – and slapped her. Then I pulled her to the front door and told her to get out. When she didn't move, I opened the door and shoved her. As she stood in the doorway, shocked at the impact, I pushed her again, more roughly this time. She fell backwards, fear crowding her face at my sudden strength.

It was then I understood why I had always resented strength. As she looked up at me, her lower lip bleeding, I felt shame wash over me. I had a flashback to my mother lying on the floor, her nose bleeding as my father towered over her. Though she never told anyone, I knew they fought all the time, my father often resorting to similar violence.

I couldn't believe it. *I had turned into the man I never wanted to be.*

Saira and Saeed

Why do we become the people we hate? Is love after all so weak that it crumbles in the face of loathing? We had four short weeks to ponder over these questions, since we had to attend weekly therapy sessions as a part of dissolving the MoC.

It was during those sessions with the therapist that we discovered the truth about our marriage and, in turn, about ourselves. It took many subsequent weeks of therapy and a lot of money for us to realize that the real marriage of convenience was the one we had made between our real and our fake selves. Between the people we had been brought up to be by our parents and the people we desired to be, there was a vast gap.

The final thing we learned from all this was that it is very difficult to love another person if you don't love yourself in the first place.

Love is not about marriage.

And marriage is not always about love.

Ghazal

Nazneen Ahmed

Rokeya stared at the thick layer of grey fluff on the tops of the boxes. She'd never opened them, from move to move, just shoved them under beds or into the back of cupboards. She had thought that taking everything with her would make the leaving final, that it would close the door to her ever returning. But now here she was, carting the boxes back to the place from which they'd come.

She let out a hiss of air through her front teeth. There wasn't much room in her Citroen, unlike her dad's Merc or the vans he would arrange from his friends' businesses. So some of these boxes would have to go. She brushed the fluff onto the floor and opened up one of them with a pair of scissors, running its sharp blade through the centre of the glossy brown tape.

Carefully, she peeled away the softened cardboard. Within were photographs, tickets, notebooks, her school shirt with multicoloured scrawled signatures, her first stethoscope.

And that's when she saw it.

A yellow and black pamphlet, folded into three hastily so that the edges didn't quite meet up. A slightly fuzzy image of a harmonium on the front, drawn with a thick pen, some musical notes, and Urdu and English written across.

In the margin, splodged sideways in liquid eyeliner, a name and a number.

Iqbal.

*

They were late, as always. Late to an event that itself had started late. That took some doing. Rokeya hated being late, but that was her father for you. The lover of attention, of drama, who wanted his entrance to cause as much disruption as possible.

He wouldn't dream of them just sneaking in round the back. Oh no. He'd swan in, loud as anything, arms outstretched for his adoring fans. He'd sorted out paperwork for them, had dealt with the police when those pigs' heads turned up at the masjid. In their small Asian community, he was the village chieftain. Never mind the poor musicians on the stage. It was him they were waiting for.

Rokeya cringed as they made their way into the church hall, which smelled of biryani mingled with floor polish and the disinfectant she remembered from primary school. Her father walked in, arms raised and wide open, as usual for these gatherings.

'Abba, please, let's just sit here,' she pleaded. 'There are two free chairs right here – look. There's no room at the front – all the seats are taken.'

'Arre, Rokeya, you are too English. They will move. Besides, they all want to wish you well now you have your results. They are your uncles. You must ask for blessings from them – after all, when will you see them again? Some of us might not even be here, the next time you are home.'

'Abba, don't be so melodramatic.'

'It's true. We don't know what's written on our foreheads, we don't know when Allah has arranged for us to pass. Come, receive their blessings. They're proud of you, their daughter.'

They were proud of her. Was that his roundabout way of saying that *he* was proud of her? If so, why couldn't he just say it, once?

'Salaam, Rahim-Saab. So nice of you and your beti to come.'

She looked up to see that a line of men – some older than her abba – were already queuing to clasp her father's hand in cupped, double palms. Rokeya pulled her jumper sleeves down over her own hands. Her mother had ironed a kameez for her, but she didn't want to feel stiff and out of place in her own body. She didn't want it to be like Eid. She just wanted to listen to the ghazals and be free. So she'd left the kameez where it had been laid, on her bed.

When she'd come down in her oversized jumper and black jeans, her father had frowned.

'You're going to wear . . . that?'

'Yes, Abba. It's too cold for a kameez. And it's covered up.'

He'd left it at that and she had been relieved. They both knew evenings such as this one didn't come to their neck of the woods all that often, and neither of them wanted a row to spoil it.

During the interval, she hung back. Her father was preoccupied with his admirers now, and she had been shown off and was of no further use to him. At last she could sit down and listen in peace.

She looked for a new seat on a row at the far back. Most of the uncles were still queuing for further helpings of food. There were very few young people here. She twisted her arms about her, and tried to remember the songs. She loved the sound, but the Urdu, the words, were lost on her. If she were Pakistani, would she have understood them? she wondered. She struggled to follow the words to Bengali songs, even though she could speak the language. It was as if the music drew a veil over the words. But it didn't really matter: the music spoke through the veil.

Someone came and sat on her row.

'Rosie . . . right?' he said.

Rokeya snapped her head up. It was years since anyone had called her that. Even her parents had finally desisted. There was a boy – no, a young man – sitting on the edge of the row. The cheek. The nerve of it! She felt all prudish, like a grandmother. She wanted to click her tongue in disapproval.

'Yes?' she said stiffly.

'Iqbal. Your dad did the accounts for my dad's restaurant when we were kids. You probably don't remember. Tariq Uncle.'

Rokeya squinted her eyes. Suddenly a rush of pungent tandoori masala hit her nose from memory. Their rooms above the restaurant had stunk of it. She remembered napkins: they used to draw dragons on the paper napkins. They'd been obsessed with them after Iqbal had taped *Dungeons and Dragons* religiously each week, and they'd watched the whole series during the summer holidays with feverish attention.

'Oh, yeah! I do remember. Iqbal.' She gave a kind of grimace. A smile wouldn't be right, not to a boy, not right here in front of all these uncles. 'Paper napkins.'

He flashed a smile.

'Yeah! Dragons. We were crazy about them. Abba used to get so mad once you were gone. But he never once thought to buy some paper so we could draw on that instead.' He gave a little laugh and looked thoughtful. Rokeya peered at the young man, lost in his memories.

The skinny, lanky boy she remembered had turned into one of those 'boyz' she mocked with her sister. Slicked, greasy curtains of hair, the too-clean trainers, the polo shirt and ugh, the worst – a chain. From the chain she knew exactly what kind of music he listened to, his worldview, and what he thought of Asian girls like herself who wore Doc Martens. But, she scolded herself, they'd drawn dragons and he remembered that. The scorn rising in her softened.

'No one calls me Rosie any more. It's Rokeya.'

'Ah, cool. Rokeya. Abba tells me you're off to university. Living away.'

She nodded.

'That's very . . . modern.'

Ugh again! He was just like the others. He was just what she thought he was. The scorn rose once more like bile within her.

'Maybe we Bangladeshis are just more advanced than you Pakistanis. You know what they say – what Bengal thinks today, the rest of the subcontinent thinks in fifty years,' she spat.

They didn't say it. Her father did.

Iqbal looked taken aback, raising his hands and protesting, 'Hey, hey – I wasn't judging.'

'Yes, you were.' Rokeya looked away, focusing intently on a noticeboard for the Girl Guides who used this hall once a week. They were raising funds to attend a Guiding convention in the United States. *America.* She couldn't wait to leave this town, where everyone knew everything about you and judged you all the time. She longed for the anonymity of the city. She kept her head firmly turned. But Iqbal didn't seem to get the message.

'I didn't mean it like that, man,' he persisted. 'It's brave. Brave of you, of your dad. My dad straight up refused. "Waste of money," he said. "Live at home, help out in the restaurant when you're not studying." Three years later, I'm still bloody here. Uni came and went, and I'm still here. I'll never leave.'

Something in his voice made Rokeya turn back to him.

'You're an adult. You're what – five years older than me? It's your life.'

'No – no, it's not.' His voice was quieter now, and his eyes serious. 'None of our lives are ours.'

Suddenly he seemed more interesting to her. There was something there, chafing at the townie uniform he wore, at the expectations. The boy who dreamed of dragons.

The lights began to dim.

'Listen, want to go for a walk?' She stood up.

'What?' He pushed his seat back, the legs scraping across the laminate. His eyes darted around as he stuffed his hands into the kangaroo pouch of his hoodie.

'Look – the music's started and the lights are down. The uncles are now full of biryani and have started to close their eyes. They won't notice. We'll be back before they know it.'

'I . . . I . . .'

Rokeya jumped up, already halfway through the door.

'Iqbal,' she said, 'you used to carve dragons on the legs of the tables in your dad's restaurant. A walk isn't remotely the worst thing you have ever done.'

*

They strolled in an awkward silence, listening to their feet on the asphalt, unsure in this new setting of where to begin again. There was a bite to the evening, and the night was darker now at nine o'clock than it would have been a few weeks ago. Rokeya pulled the extra-long jumper sleeves over her fingers and upped her pace to keep warm.

'What did you do at uni?' she asked.

'Business and Finance. Abba thought it'd help the business.'

He was a bit breathless, she noticed, amused. He probably had a car and wasn't used to walking anywhere any more. His trainers were pristinely white.

'And you?' she said. 'Is that what you wanted?'

'Does it matter?' He sounded desperate.

'Yes, Iqbal, it does.'

'It's the past. I'm well into my Accountancy exams now.'

'You're only twenty-three. Your life isn't over yet. It can't be.'

'It's just a different life. The responsible life.'

'Are they proud?'

'Who?'

'Your parents.'

There was a silence. She stopped and saw he was behind her, standing still, looking at the ground.

'Iqbal?'

'I've failed my exams three times. I got a 2:2 – just. I had to repeat a year.'

'Oh.'

She went to walk towards him but he seemed to shake himself and looked up, his eyes weirdly bright.

'You're off to do Medicine. The Asian Dream. Your Abba's so proud.'

She shrugged.

'I never had you down, back then,' he added. 'As a science nerd.'

She turned around and started to walk. 'Well, I never had you down as a mediocre Business and Finance student,' she muttered.

She began to have that feeling again, of walls closing in, of her lungs compressing. Expectations, assumptions, duty: her fluid, free self being squashed down into a respectable box. She walked faster, as if by doing so she could outrun it.

Iqbal had to jog lightly to catch up.

'Aren't you excited?' he asked. 'You don't seem excited.'

She didn't say anything, just kept walking. Boot crunching asphalt, boot crunching asphalt, she looked at her home town with a concentration she rarely gave it. It wasn't a scenic town. Not the kind of place one took evening strolls in. It was the kind of place you tried to ignore as you moved from A to B. A 'New Town' (the newness long since chipped away like the edges of a Formica table), it was designed with efficiency in mind. Efficiency, utility, minimizing costs. No one had thought about what makes a place liveable. A life liveable. Rokeya thought grimly that Asian parents might have designed it.

They came upon the playground, sandwiched between two mini-roundabouts. Rokeya said, exasperated, 'How can this be the best location for a playground?' She addressed her question to the Grand Architect in the Sky more than to anyone else. 'How?' Then: 'Uff! I can't wait to leave this place.'

Iqbal looked confused. 'What's wrong with it? We used to play here once.'

'There's no trees, the cars roar past all the time. There's no flipping grass!' She jabbed an accusing finger at the black tarmac.

'It's better than nothing.' Iqbal opened the gate. It screeched in protest, as if trying to alert the authorities to over-twelves entering.

'Your problem, Iqbal, is that you don't have any imagination.' Her voice came out too sharply.

Iqbal was already at the swings, his back to her. 'You're right, I don't – not any more. Imagination just makes you miserable for what can't be.'

She felt something lurch within her. Guilt. But also surprise. She wanted to reach out to him, but he seemed miles away. She could see the outline of his fists gripping the chain-links of the swing.

She walked quietly over to him. 'I get it. I do,' she said.

He gave a bitter laugh. 'You couldn't, Rosie. You've already imagined yourself out of here.'

'I wanted to go to art school, Iqbal. Art. School.'

He turned to her. 'What?'

'I wanted to go to art school. But Abba – for all his love of the arts, hah – said there was no point to it. "Get serious," he said, "or get married".'

21

'People don't just drift into med school, Rosie. You had to work for it. You had to want it.'

'Med school was the only way I'd ever have been able to live away. I wanted to leave more than I wanted to paint. I found the furthest med schools and applied for those. I'm going to Aberdeen. At least I'll be good at dissection drawings.'

His brow twitched with concern and he looked straight into her eyes. In the moonlight his eyes were almost hazel, she realized. It made her catch her breath and she had to look away.

'Rosie. Seven years is a big commitment to something you don't really want.'

'Aren't you on year five now?'

Iqbal gave a sheepish grin and sat down on the swing, feet planted on the tarmac, swinging gently.

'Look at us. The good, obedient, miserable Muslim kids.'

Rokeya stood in front of him. She bit her lip, and put one hand around the chain-links of the swing. It was still warm from where Iqbal had gripped it. She felt it trying to twist away from her, to follow the motion of the swing. She held firm.

'You could leave too.'

'And go where?'

'Anywhere, Iqbal. Far enough so they can't fetch you back. America. Leave them a note to say you're fine, and just go. Go on: I dare you.' The swinging stopped. Iqbal was shaking his head in wonder.

'You're crazy, Rosie. That's the craziest thing I've ever heard.'

The chain started to tug again as Iqbal pushed back on the swing to get off. Rokeya put her hand on the other chain, blocking him in.

'It's crazy, okay. But not impossible. You've got a passport –
and I bet you've got the funds. You just need the will.'

Iqbal laughed, saying, 'Imagination, man. It's not just
unhealthy, it's downright dangerous.' But there was a gleam
in his eye, the same one he'd had when they'd hidden under
the polyester tablecloths and taken turns with the penknife to
carve the first dragon. He was tempted, she could tell.

She felt a rush of something like impatience, boldness. She
touched his shoulder.

'Come on, Iqbal. It'd be an adventure. Your dad – my dad –
they had theirs, when they came here. Untied, unmarried, who
knows what they got up to. You deserve adventures too. Then
you can come back, get married to a nice Pakistani girl, and
you'll have it to look back on. The time you were happy.'

He looked at her hand on his shoulder. Carefully, he put his
hand over hers.

'Rosie,' he said softly. 'I used to be happy.'

He touched her face with a crooked finger. Rokeya felt numb
and simultaneously as though every particle of her skin under
his touch were supercharged. She held her breath.

*

Nine years. Nine whole years ago. She'd been full of hope,
despite everything. And now the escape she'd traded her dreams
for was reaching its expiry date. She was going home. Amma
couldn't manage on her own.

She put the box by the bin. No point taking these memories
with her where they'd only taunt her. She told herself that it
would be fine. She was older now – a doctor no less, a GP, and

despite everything, she did love it. It wasn't painting, but there was creativity in it, she'd discovered. Listening, building trust, thinking up solutions to her patients' problems. She'd still have that. And yet, she felt the feeling rising again – the feeling she'd tried to outrun these past nine years but which always came back, however far away she went. The feeling that stopped her from opening the boxes.

She played with the pamphlet in her hands, rolling it up, unfolding it. The photocopied black lines began to wear away.

She remembered the kiss, there in that playground, like delinquent alcohol-swilling teenagers. It had been her first.

There was no point in calling him. Who even had the same number after nine years, anyway? He was probably married, probably had kids. While she, she had got the Dr in front of her name, and the MBBS at the end.

She folded up the pamphlet. She had made him write his number down, even though she didn't have a pen, even though, as he wrote the numbers carefully, blowing on the ink, they knew neither of them would speak again.

But now she was going back. Maybe she'd visit the restaurant. Pay her respects to her uncle. It had to still be there.

She pulled her laptop out to check. What was it called again? She cast her mind back to the acrid hit of tandoori masala, the paper boats, the dragons on the table legs. It was one of those names of its time. After a while they all merged into one: the Raj Tandoori, the Taj Mahal, the Bengal.

The Bengal! Her father had found it ever-hilarious, a Pakistani-owned restaurant called the Bengal.

'Didn't you take enough from us when we were your colony?' he had joshed with Iqbal's father, who had simply shrugged jovially in return.

It didn't come up immediately. There was, or rather had been, only a handful of Indian restaurants in their town, so it should have been right at the top, in the list of online takeaways.

She scrolled. On Google Maps it was marked 'Closed'. Her stomach dipped with sadness. She knew that those old-school restaurants with their flocked wallpaper were fading away, but she had thought Iqbal's might survive. There was no telling where he or his family might be now, unless she asked Amma. And Amma would wonder why she was asking after the Pakistani restaurant wallah's boy.

She wondered what had taken the Bengal's place. Maybe luxury flats, now the New Town was finally being absorbed into London's spread. She scrolled Maps and clicked on the yellow star that marked the location, half-wondering what on earth she was doing, sleuthing like this.

It hadn't been turned into flats.

Where the Bengal had been once was a restaurant called Naga. 'Modern Indo-Chinese fusion', Google told her. The star rating was high.

She clicked on it to look at its crisp black and red frontage.

And then she smiled.

Curled around the Indic font was a dragon.

Her Trials

Mariam Naeem

Her smile widened as she fumbled in her bag for her keys, elated at the prospect of being home before Gabriel for once. Aliyah thought about what she could make for dinner, or whether she and Gabe would end up just going out for the evening. There was a new Vietnamese restaurant she had been planning to try. Either way, it would be fun. Their three-year anniversary was less than a month away, so that would also require some planning on her part. She turned the key in the lock, pushing the door wide open.

The place seemed silent. After locking the door again behind her, she walked in and put her bag on the sideboard. She went still as she heard a faint giggle. Probably the TV that Gabriel had left on. Aliyah walked towards the living room located at the end of the hallway. When she reached its glass door and looked through, her eyes widened in shock at the tawdry sight before her, and she felt as though she'd just been drenched in icy water. Tears began to stream down her face, tracking faint lines through the makeup on her cheeks. Her heart thumped loudly as the pain of what she was seeing coursed through her.

There, on the sofa, was Gabriel. But he was not alone. The giggling she had heard wasn't from the television as she had assumed. It was coming from a beautiful brunette tangled in her husband's arms. They were kissing and the woman kept laughing every time Gabriel said something that amused her.

The keys that Aliyah still held fell from her hand, jingling as they hit the wooden floor.

Gabriel jumped up and pushed the woman away. Looking around for the source of the noise, he stopped moving once he saw her – a thief captured in security lights. His own eyes widened in horror at the realization that he'd been caught. His eyes, those beautiful blue eyes, gaped at her while his cheeks flushed red. His hair was tousled, no longer neatly combed as it had been that morning when he left for work.

Her heart ached as she looked at him. Why?

*

After the other woman had skulked out of the house and she and Gabriel were left alone, Aliyah found she was incapable of speaking to him and instead retreated to the bedroom.

Their bedroom. With their clothes, their bed. She stared at it, wondering if he had brought the woman upstairs before. With that thought, her remaining resolve faded as she crumpled and sank to the floor beside the dressing table, a hand over her mouth to stifle her sobs, trying not to let Gabriel hear.

Three years. Had it all been a lie? How long had it been going on? She couldn't deal with seeing his face or staying in this house any longer. She didn't want to think about him and the other woman here in their home, in their bed. The worst part was that it was *her* house, with her name on the deeds.

Once the tears stopped, a numb feeling settled itself in her chest. She tore into her closet space, grabbing things quickly and throwing them all into a suitcase. She would only take what she needed, she decided. Her sister Safiyah could come around to pack up her home and tell Gabriel he had to leave. Aliyah didn't want to see him. She didn't need to – she only wanted to get rid of the bad memories. And that meant the house too.

As she was finishing her packing, she heard the front door slam shut. That must mean Gabriel didn't want to talk either, she thought. Aliyah grew furious and her packing became increasingly frantic out of her desperation to leave. She needed to see her sister.

*

'How dare he! The disgusting, filthy animal!'

Aliyah supposed her sister's rage was better than an expression of pity. 'Look, Safiyah, I don't want to make a big fuss of this,' she said. 'I just want to end it.'

'Of course you do. He's so stupid! And I'm not just saying that because I'm your sister. I actually thought you two had something amazing. Mum was always telling me to find someone like Gabriel. Well, hopefully she won't think the sun shines out of his arse any more now. The stupid idiot.'

Aliyah held on tightly to her coffee cup. Starbucks was busy and she didn't want to look up and meet anyone's eye, somehow afraid they might see her for the fool she had been.

She still didn't understand. What had happened? Why had he cheated? There was nothing wrong with their relationship, was there? Well, she didn't think so. Conversations were always continuous and never awkward. The sex was great. She enjoyed going out with him because they got on so well. They could communicate. He never seemed to flirt with other women and had always appeared totally dedicated to her. What had gone wrong?

'Aliyah, stop it. I can see your cogs turning. You're overthinking the situation. At the end of the day he's a man. And men tend to cheat. They can't help it.'

Safiyah's voice washed over her and she closed her eyes, her forehead resting against the warm cup.

'Look, Jay-Z had the cheek to mess Beyoncé about. I mean, Beyoncé! The sexiest woman on the planet and he did that to her for someone who was just plain. Men don't care. I sound harsh but I'm right.'

A man who had been staring at his phone for the past ten minutes looked over, affronted. 'Excuse me, but not all men are like that. You can't lump us all together.'

Safiyah looked at him, her eyes narrowing. 'Can't I? Tell me, are you in a relationship? Is that the woman you're texting at the moment? Because you're smiling quite a lot and looking pleased with yourself.'

The man spluttered. 'Look, that is beside the point. I could be texting a friend.'

Safiyah gave a lofty shrug and rolled her eyes. 'But you're not, are you?'

Aliyah was mortified. Her sister was having an argument with a complete stranger about cheating, and making accusations. She wished the coffee cup was large enough to swallow her.

'Maybe I am texting another woman, but my relationship is none of your business.' With that, the man stormed out, sending a last death glare to Safiyah, who waved at him sarcastically.

She turned to Aliyah. 'Looks like I was right. Did you see his face? He knew he'd been caught!' She was about to continue speaking but stopped at her sister's stricken expression. She leaned over and gently touched Aliyah's hand. 'Maybe we should go home? We can watch a bunch of trashy movies on Netflix and binge on ice cream. Just for tonight, though. We are going to the gym tomorrow and then the spa. No disagreement allowed.'

'That's fine. Let's go.' Aliyah's insides felt heavy.

*

Sitting across from her mother, watching her reaction, had made her feel that it was her fault Gabriel had cheated. It was now two weeks since it had happened.

'Did you respect him enough? Give him enough space? Did you cook for him? Give him what he asked for when you had private time?'

'Mum! I did nothing but love that man. We were so good together. You don't understand. *I* don't understand! Why would he do this to me? You think I made him cheat? That I pushed him away? Well, I didn't. I didn't do anything that could possibly make him cheat.'

'No, honey, I just meant . . .'

'I know what you meant. Telling me I was a shit wife and didn't give him everything, when I did! You're supposed to support me, not him. He's in the wrong! If I'd been the one cheating, I could understand. What gives you the right to judge me anyway? You stayed with Dad all those years when you knew he was seeing that other woman behind your back. For years! And you want me to be the same? I don't think so!'

Aliyah's mother raised a hand, stopping her daughter's outburst. 'Relationships are difficult at the best of times. We need to be there for each other. We need to support each other. We need to show them that even though they have messed up, we're still there, and we always will be. Have you even spoken to him since you caught him? Sat down to discuss it like adults? Find out why he did what he did? I want you to call him. At the very least, you need answers. You need closure. Or you'll become bitter. I never questioned your father about Veronica and I've always regretted it. But I stayed with him, yes. I loved him for all those years. We work at our marriages. We don't leave at the sign of a little infidelity. Go, talk to him. Try reconciling. The whole family will be devastated to learn you've split.'

'No! I don't care what the family think. I won't stay with a man who has the nerve to do that to me.' Aliyah paced the room frantically, trying to calm her breathing. 'That might be the pressure you had to face when you were younger but I'm not subjecting myself to it. It'd be torture! I'll never stay with a man who can't love and respect me. An unfaithful man is someone I can't trust.'

Aliyah stopped and sat back down, tears welling up in her eyes, burying her face in her hands. 'Why wasn't I enough for him?'

She felt hollow. Her whole chest ached. She felt she was constantly falling, further and further down. The stable ground beneath her had been ripped away in a single moment. What if she hadn't finished work early? Would she never have caught them? Lived her life in ignorant bliss?

Aliyah's mother sighed, and then Aliyah felt her mum's hand gently smoothing her hair. 'I only want you to be happy. It's just that I know what the pressure of everyone's negative thoughts can do to you. I'd rather you didn't go through that. Try talking to him first.'

*

Two days later and Aliyah gave in to her mother. She sent Gabriel a text asking him to meet her at her favourite spot in the park. There, a small bench overlooked the pond, which was enveloped by weeping willows and taken over by small ducks, quacking, waddling and swimming. She liked it for being out of the way and so peaceful. It was always a good place to gather her thoughts.

As she waited for him, Aliyah thought about all those times she had finished work and got home to find him waiting for her, a happy expression on his face. Lies. All of it.

She didn't want to get emotional when she saw him. She definitely didn't want him to know she had been crying herself to sleep each night. So she had decided on what she called a 'power outfit'. Casual, but powerful to her. She had paired indigo skinny jeans with a plain white tank top. Over that, she wore a new cropped black leather jacket. Around her neck was a simple gold necklace, with the Egyptian Ankh as a pendant. On her feet she wore a pair of low-heeled black shoes as she hated being too high off the ground. Spiky studs trailed along the back of them and down the heel, looking menacing in this light. She had kept her makeup natural. The only dramatic effect was her eyeliner, with its deadly-looking point that lent her a fierce glare. She needed it. Needed the confidence boost the winged eyeliner gave her. She wore her hair in a high, sleek ponytail. Her favourite black handbag, with its own small sprinkling of metal studs, completed the kick-ass look. She thought her outfit got across the point that she was not to be messed with, but respected and admired.

Aliyah had been so busy focusing on her heels and pointing one toe at the pond, trying to get herself in the right frame of mind for this talk, that she was startled when she noticed Gabriel standing in front of her, wearing a pained look. On closer inspection, Aliyah saw he hadn't shaved. His shirt and trousers were a little rumpled, as though he had slept in them. He had dark shadows under his eyes, so maybe he too had been losing sleep. She almost felt sorry for him, but then his phone rang, pulling them both out of the moment.

Aliyah saw the expression on Gabriel's face as he saw the caller's name, and knew what he would do even before he did. She knew him. It was a call he didn't want to get at that moment – a call he had probably been avoiding for a while. She also knew who it was. She watched him fumble with the phone, struggling to switch it off and put it in his pocket, before he sat down next to her.

He just sat there. Neither of them spoke; tension thickened the air.

Aliyah decided she should speak first. She had no wish to prolong this agony. 'Are you still living at the house?' she asked, and closed her eyes as the image of their home worked its way into her mind. Then she shook her head slightly, trying to dispel this vision.

'I moved out last week, Aliyah. I waited for you to come back, but when you sent Safiyah round to tell me to clear off, I knew you weren't coming back.' His voice was soft.

'Well, why would you assume I'd come back after watching my husband getting it on with some random slut in *my own house*? Not only that: why did you leave instead of trying to explain your sorry ass? What made you think I'd go running back to you after you betrayed me?'

Aliyah's voice was sharp, ensuring she drove each barb home so he understood her.

'Tell me why you were with her and how many other times there have been. Was it just her, or were there more women? We had it so good and you decided to destroy it. I was planning our anniversary – and all the time you were fucking around behind my back! Do you know what you've done to me? Do you care?'

'Of course I care! That's why I'm here. I'm here to explain. I *will* explain.' He ran his hands through his hair in frustration. 'Look, it was a bad decision on my part. I shouldn't have brought her home.'

'How long have you been seeing her?' Aliyah stared intently at him, trying to gauge his expression.

'I work with her. We've gone out to business lunches together and that work trip I went on to France, she came along too. We were in the same hotel, but we had separate rooms.'

'Hang on, that trip was three months ago. Are you telling me you've been seeing her for three months? Three months? But that means . . .' Aliyah's voice trailed off as she processed the realization that he hadn't spent her birthday working as she had thought. She felt sick. She had spent that night with her mother and sister while he had been cheating on her in France. He had told her he couldn't miss the trip. That it was too important for the team.

'I know, I'm really sorry. I didn't mean to. It just happened. When I got back to England, I ended it right there and then. But then I had a shitty day at work and Lara was there. We went to a bar around the corner from the office, to talk about work, nothing else. But it happened again. You have every right to hate me. I hate myself for putting you through this. You didn't deserve me doing this to you.'

Gabriel turned to look at Aliyah, his eyes pleading. 'Things just haven't been right since we split. Things have gone dark. I've left my job. I've applied for a new one, it'd pay better, and I wouldn't be working as many hours. I'm renting my own place now on the other side of the city. I'm really trying here to show you I've been working on changing.'

Aliyah's voice was low. 'Where did you stay last night, Gabriel?'

Gabriel took a sharp breath in. 'Aliyah, please. I was at home. I swear.'

'Don't lie to me. I don't understand why you can't be honest. You're wearing the same clothes as yesterday. I know because I saw a photo of you on Instagram yesterday in these clothes, in a bar, with a woman next to you. And before you ask, no, I wasn't snooping. When you get drunk you start taking and posting a lot of photos. You always have done. But you sometimes tag me in them. And you did that last night. You want to tell me you've changed. You're telling me you've quit your job. Got a new place. Looks like you also got something else that's new.'

Aliyah stood abruptly. 'Give me the ring, Gabriel.'

He jumped back in the bench, his right hand closing over the left, covering his wedding band. 'You can't be serious?'

'I've heard everything I need to. I have no idea why, but it seems you never wanted me by your side for the rest of your life. It seems you didn't want to start that family. To celebrate our anniversary. To love me. I get it.' Aliyah's voice was choked with emotion.

She took a deep breath, knowing that what she was about to do next would hurt her more than it would hurt him. She knew she would look melodramatic, even a little crazy, but it would drive her point home. It would finish it. She looked at him as she pulled her ring off her finger. She twirled it between her fingers for a moment, looking at it for the last time. Then, glancing contemptuously at his face, Aliyah spun round to face the pond. She trembled a little, then threw the ring. It made a small splash as it landed in the water. She picked up her handbag and placed it in the crook of her arm before walking away, head held high.

*

Aliyah lay face down on the massage table, resigned to her fate. Safiyah lay on the table next to her. As the masseuse kneaded her back gently, she sighed. And then the tears began to flow.

'Aliyah! Aliyah, we are here to relax. Getting worked up won't help you. Do it afterwards. I promise you need this.' Safiyah reached her hand over and took a few swipes before finding her sister's and grabbing it tightly. 'It's okay. You did what you had to do. You're so brave. To be honest, I'd have gone out and done far worse after finding out something like that. Good job I'm single. I don't need a man messing up my life. My wardrobe.'

Aliyah let out a small chuckle and sniffed again. Her sister was in love with her wardrobe and with fashion. She owned and ran a successful clothing boutique, in which most of the clothes were designed by her. Naturally, her wardrobe was her pride and joy. It took up three bedrooms in her house. The fourth was her office. The fifth, a small studio for photo shoots. The sixth was her own. Aliyah was proud of Safiyah. She had worked hard to live her dream of a house filled with clothes. She would never let a man enter her home. Nothing could replace her work.

'You don't understand, Safiyah. I don't think he even meant anything he said at the park. I've been ignoring him. I've blocked him on social media. I'm trying to move on. And you keep showing me those stupid photos he's been uploading, the ones of him with all those women in the bars. It all proves my point. And it really hurts that I'm right.'

'Ouch!' Safiyah nudged her masseuse's hands. 'Be gentle! Look, Aliyah, you were right. And no, it's not going to be easy. But you're already working on freeing yourself. You've already put your house on the market. Mum's here for you and so am I. We aren't leaving your side.'

Aliyah's voice quietened almost to a whisper. 'I miss him, I really do. But I hate him so much. It hurts every time I think of him. It hurts when I drive to work and see his old office. It hurts worse whenever I'm at home. I'm alone. I don't like it, but I'm learning to deal with it. I'm trying to make the hurt go away but it doesn't work all the time. I even started yoga – I thought it might help.'

'Well, hon, you know I told you at least a year ago you needed to start yoga. It's fantastic. If you feel lonely, call me. I'm only an hour away. And besides, sleepovers never get old, do they?'

Aliyah's masseuse piped up, 'Get a bunch of your friends around, darling, and throw a big party. Girls only. Good times only. Make sure you invite me too, though. You need friends around you. And family.'

Safiyah laughed. 'I never say no to a party. I know you don't feel like one, but a girls' night in could be just what you need. If you don't want to go out, we can come to you. No more ice cream and Netflix binges. Good times only from now.'

Aliyah's heart lifted a little at the words of support. She'd tried seeing a therapist but it hadn't worked. She had left in floods of tears, convinced that she was the cause of Gabriel doing what he did.

Maybe Safiyah and the masseuse were right. A girls' night in. A party. She didn't want to be alone in her house. This could help her accept that Gabriel was never going to change.

Her marriage was over.

Boneland

Shaista Sadick

*He plunged his rigid shaft directly into her moist centre,
like a mighty sword of faith thrust into the heart of an
unbeliever . . .*

'We're nearly out of toilet paper. Is there any more?' Jamie came
into the kitchen, still in his pyjamas, yawning, and scratching at
his belly in a half-hearted manner.

'Check in the cabinet under the sink.' *He plunged his rigid
shaft . . .*

'I already did.'

Sania turned around and frowned. 'Then why ask? You'll
have to go to the shop.'

He plunged his . . .

He walked towards her, full of bedhead and early morning
breath, his stubble more salt than pepper these days, and she
tried not to wince as he leaned forward and kissed her cheek,
nearly knocking her coffee onto her laptop and papers. She

pushed her cup to one side and straightened the papers. 'It's your turn to drive the girls to school.'

'I know.'

'I'm just reminding you, because in the past you've made them late.'

'It was only once, Sania. I wish you would let it go.' He moved to the counter and poured himself a cup of coffee, his back turned.

'It's just . . . I need to finish this story before the girls get home this afternoon.'

'All right. I'll jump in the shower.'

She let him go. She was hard on him these days, she knew. But it was difficult. She needed the time to focus, and he never seemed to understand that, or understand what a burden it was to be the only breadwinner in the family.

Once the girls were up, it would be impossible to write. There would be breakfast and squabbles and missing homework and more squabbles and a lost PE kit and even more squabbles about whose turn it was to feed the hamster . . . And Jamie would do what Jamie always did. He'd disappear into himself.

He rested his face in the cleft between her beautiful twin towers . . .

Hmm . . . perhaps not.

She feasted on him like he was iftar . . .

The screaming began and she slammed her laptop shut, looking behind her. Naila had a clump of Mona's hair in her fist, while the younger girl was the one screaming as they barrelled down the stairs like attached marionettes.

'Stop it!'

'I'm not doing anything.'

'Maammaa, she's hurting me!'

'She started it! She took my phone and read all my texts. She has no respect for my privacy. And it's your fault, for not letting me put a password on my phone!'

'Let go of your sister's hair, Naila,' Sania said quietly. 'Now, please.'

With a push and a lurch, Mona was free. She glared daggers at Naila. 'I didn't look at your phone. You're always accusing me, when *you're* the one who goes through my stuff all the time. Mama, *tell* her!'

But Naila had moved on. She was biting into an apple now, while simultaneously opening the fridge door and hunting around for her packed lunch. 'Oh, please,' she said between chews. 'There's absolutely nothing about your life that interests me.'

Sania zoned out the noise. She got up to prepare breakfast . . . Well, for Mona and Jamie at least. Only yoghurt for Naila. When Sania had gone to Sainsbury's yesterday they hadn't had the Fruit Corner ones her daughter liked, so it had to be pre-blended strawberry, though of course Naila would baulk at that.

She drew a long breath. These days, she spent half the mornings trying to strengthen herself against her daughter's eye-rolls. She looked at Naila's waif-like figure. She was worried that the girl was developing body issues, she ate so little . . .

The butter sizzled in the pan and she focused on the task at hand. Scrambled eggs for Mona, who was now complaining about not having a phone of her own. The kids ate, and Jamie came down looking almost human in his smart–casual attire, his hair still glistening from the shower.

This time, when he kissed her, she kissed him back. She got a juicy hug from Mona, a breezy 'See ya!' from Naila – the phrase was loaded with the expected amount of ennui – and then, just like that, it was over.

The kitchen was silent. Mona had forgotten her jumper. Naila had left a half-eaten yoghurt on the counter, tilted and oozing strawberry. Neither had put their plates in the dishwasher. Sania fought the urge to tidy up, and sat down once more at the laptop.

He plunged his rigid shaft directly into her moist centre . . . No, she had tried that line already.

There was a jihad going on in his pants, and when she ripped off her burqa, he saw that she was worth giving up his seventy-two virgins for . . . Nope, that wasn't going to work either.

She leaned back and sighed. It should be easier than this by now. This was her seventeenth story, bugger it. The first one had taken less than an hour to write, but it seemed to get progressively harder. Perhaps because now there was real money at stake, or perhaps she had simply run out of euphemisms. She poured herself another coffee.

She cupped her hands around the mug, enjoying its warmth. That first story had been a piss-take, which was probably why it had been so easy, she decided. Her friend Becky had come across the website, Boneland.net: The World's Number One Halal Erotica. It was mostly made up of fan fiction about the TV show *Homeland*: a Fifty Shades of Terrorism type of thing. One drunken night at a wine bar they had dared each other to submit stories under pseudonyms. When Sania's was actually accepted, neither of them could get over it. For weeks they had giggled about the accolade, until Sania received a payment of £350. Payment was based on the number of clicks her story received, and she had thousands. Someone had actually *paid* her to write a story about Abu Broudieh, the double agent with his hard, male heat and his engorged flesh.

No one was more stunned than she was when the story topped the website's rankings. It had been a joke, for God's sake! And then one of the editors of Boneland contacted her to ask if she could provide any more submissions. She hated her freelance copywriting job, and thought, Why not?

She decided to give it a go. A little extra pocket money on the side, on top of what she was already earning. Jamie had not been happy.

'It's . . . Well, it's not that I mind the erotica, darling. It's just . . . Muslim erotica?'

'What about it?'

'It's racist, my love. All these stories about terrorists bonking women in hijabs and making them submit to their every whim. It's . . . Well, I think it verges on hate speech, actually. It's misogynistic too.'

This was so typical of Jamie. Always so politically correct. When she had introduced him to her parents, he arrived dressed in a shalwar kameez, all eager to acknowledge his white privilege and to discuss the best way to cook haleem, even though her father was a bank manager and her mother an accountant who much preferred a little salad over anything too heavy. 'No more so than *Fifty Shades*,' she shot back. 'It's kinky, a fetish. Like men who wear nappies and want to be spanked.'

'Do you know any such men?'

'No. At least, I don't think so.'

'Would you like it if I wore a nappy to bed?'

'Don't be gross.'

'Well, there you go then.'

But that had been three months ago. Two weeks later, Jamie had lost his teaching job, and her freelancing money could only stretch so far. He picked up bits and pieces of tutoring, but schools were having budget crises, and nobody seemed to care about the Plantagenets quite as much as he did. The world had moved on, and yet Jamie seemed to be from another age. All his desperate attempts to embrace her culture only reminded her that he was so *English*.

His breath was heavy against her mouth. 'I'm going to explode inside you like a suicide bomber,' he whispered . . .

When Jamie lost his job, she wrote a second story, about a Mata Hari-type female spy who infiltrated ISIS and got caught, finding herself forced into a group orgy. It was one of her most popular – she made £1200 off it. Since then, she had never looked back.

'Just think about it, darling, that's all I'm saying. What kind of man wants to read stuff like this? By the way, have you seen my glasses? I'm sure I left them in the bedroom, but I can't find them. I bet Mona's hidden them again. I really wish she would stop being so silly. We have to start thinking about her birthday, by the way. Any idea of what she wants?'

'Well, maybe they're women . . .'

'What?'

'The readership. Maybe they're women.'

'I highly doubt it.'

'Well, either way, stop being such a prude.'

Eventually, he gave in and just ignored her new source of income. When Mona turned out to have dyslexia, it was *Her Holy Gyrations* that paid for extra tuition to help her catch up with the rest of the class. When Naila wanted to go on a school skiing trip, and when Jamie himself needed to see a professional CV consultant, it was the stories, always the stories, that came through for them.

Sania didn't put much effort into her prose, but it turned out she had a knack for writing Islamic terror erotica. She'd accidentally become the queen of a whole new subset of porn, and she could churn the stories out almost as fast as her readers devoured them.

Her readers . . . When she thought about them, she would picture her overweight cousin Javaid, who worked at the EE store on the Edgware Road and ate McDonald's for lunch every day. He consumed porn like it was air, all the while making sick comments about women in miniskirts. Javaid's mother was looking for a pious girl to marry him off to, and he himself had announced that she had to be a virgin who knew how to cook. It would help if she were a doctor or a nurse, he added, so that she could look after his parents in their old age. And of course, she had to be from Pakistan, because otherwise she wouldn't understand his culture.

Sania liked to think she was making money off idiots like him.

But today the story just wasn't coming to her. A walk might be a good idea. She could buy some loo roll and clear her head at the same time. Plus, she had to get some craft paper for Mona's map of the world project, and some macaroni which, for unfathomable reasons, was going to represent the Himalayas.

Twenty minutes later, she found herself embracing the smells and sights of Kilburn High Road, a canvas shopping bag on her shoulder. She passed the halal butchers and gazed briefly into the window of the Primark store, wondering if it was worth buying another pair of trainers – the last ones had disintegrated during their summer holiday in France. Better to buy a pair that would last, she decided, and moved on. She stopped at the fruit stall, where they were still selling cardboard boxes of mangoes – and that made her think about Jamie.

She'd first met Jamie at her friend Becky's twenty-third birthday party, almost a quarter of a century ago. He had a teaching assistant job, working at a secondary school in Cricklewood, and she had just graduated with an English degree which turned out to be utterly useless. They'd bonded over their love of Nirvana and Doc Martens, and shared hatred of boybands and the Macarena. The next day he rang Sania, who was staying with Becky, and asked if she fancied a walk. They had talked and walked the length and breadth of north London. She'd introduced him to Pakistani mangoes, and he was so delighted by them that he bought a crate a week for the entire season.

Dating white guys had never been her thing, but Jamie was smart, and funny, and didn't seem to care how many men she might or might not have slept with. After he entered her life, she began to feel it was no longer possible for her to continue living with her parents in Croydon, surrounded by judgemental aunties and arrogant boys . . . And girls who married too young and gave up their careers.

Jamie was steady and calm, and his green eyes crinkled at the edges when he smiled. He was the best kind of nerd, the sort of person who would open doors for strangers and spend his holidays exploring old castles. It didn't matter to him whether her parents were active in the community, or whether she said her prayers. It didn't matter that she drank, or smoked, or intended to live off Heinz Baked Beans for the rest of her life instead of learning how to cook. He made her laugh, all the time, and he let her laugh *at* him too, when he dragged her to some particularly damp and dusty ruin and lectured her about Richard I.

There was a chill to the air. She walked home laden with mangoes, macaroni, toilet paper and the right kind of yoghurt for Naila. She made her way into the kitchen and dumped everything on the table. Jamie had come and gone, it seemed, because the kitchen had been cleaned and the whole house was gleaming. On the counter was a roll of toilet paper. And in the middle of the roll, a single red rose.

She smiled, and went back to her story.

She soared over the crest in a frenzy of simultaneous explosions, those within her, and those outside, where the ISIS fighters had gathered.

An email pinged from her Gmail account, and she opened it immediately, curious. It was from one of the editors of Boneland, she knew, because they were the only ones who had her personal address. They knew her surname and bank details, of course, but everything else was anonymized. Her moniker, Desigirl73, was not in any way original, but that's what she liked about it.

Hi Desigirl73!
Thank you for all your submissions so far. We've recently added new functionality to the site, as well as raising our subscription fee. Readers are now able to like and comment on stories, and we've had a lot of

feedback already. Could we talk? My details are below,
if you have time to call me.
Sincerely,
Andrew Marsh

Sania sat back. She had never had a conversation with
anyone from the site before; she didn't even know where it was
headquartered. Andrew had provided a US number. She rang it
before she could change her mind.

'This is Andrew,' said the voice, in lieu of a hello.

'Oh. Hi. This is San . . . er . . . you know me as Desigirl73,
I guess?'

'Oh, hey!' His tone brightened. 'It's so nice to hear from
you. How *are* you today?'

She never knew how to deal with over-enthusiastic
Americans, and this one had a Midwestern inflection to boot.
It struck her just then that she knew very little about Boneland.

'I am well, thank you. And yourself?'

'Oh, I'm great. Just great! Thanks for calling me back. As I
said in my email, we've made some upgrades to the site . . .'

'Yes?'

'And I gotta tell you, our readers are just lovin' your stories.'

That was good, she thought. 'That's good.'

'Uh huh. But the thing is, they'd like some more diversity.'

'Diversity? In what way?'

'Well . . . all your characters are Mozlem, right?'

'Yes. Erm, isn't that the whole point?' Why was a guy named
Andrew, who couldn't say the word Muslim properly, running
a website for Muslim erotica? She started a Google search,
looking up Boneland and Andrew Marsh.

He chuckled. 'Yeah, I totally get where you're coming from. But our readers want to feel like they're invested, you know? So the characters need to represent them, a little bit.'

'I see.' It was a fair point. So many of her characters were spies or terrorists, which clearly the readership wasn't. 'And how do I do that, exactly?'

'Can you throw in some American GIs? I mean, the girls have to be Mozlems, of course. But the guys, they could be saving 'em from wherever they're from, and the girls could be showing 'em how grateful they are. Like in Iraq after Saddam, but more current. What do you think? We're confident the click rate will go up; you'll make a lotta cash, and our readers will be happy. I don't know if you've seen our new competitor EroticExotic, but they've really captured the horny hijab-girl market, and that's a wake-up call for us, to be honest with you.'

An image had appeared on her screen from her search. Boneland and Andrew Marsh. There he was, wearing jeans and a check shirt – lean, sandy-haired, handsome, and grinning with his arms crossed over his chest. On his head he wore a baseball cap which said **MAKE AMERICA GREAT AGAIN**.

She took a moment to think about what she should say, but found she hadn't any words. 'I'll certainly consider that, thanks,' she said and hung up the phone.

And then she called Jamie.

'So it turns out that men wearing nappies was the least of the crazy,' she said.

'Is this your way of telling me I was right?'

'You're never right, you should know that by now. But yes.'

'Well,' he exhaled. 'It sounds like we're going to be broke again tomorrow. Shall we celebrate with a takeaway tonight? What do you fancy?'

'Chinese.'

'Okay. But just not that spicy Sichuan place you like so much. You know it goes right through me, darling. I mean, I understand how important chillies are in your culture, but we only have the one bathroom and all. Maybe they could put the chillies on the side . . .'

'Jamie?'

'Yes, love?'

'Just come home.'

'Already here, darling,' he said, as she heard the latch on the front door turn.

Tears and Tantrums

Sufiya Ahmed

'What have I done wrong?'

It is an age-old question. What have I done to lose my husband's interest? Have I put on weight without noticing? Have the lines crept up around my eyes? What is it?

Except I am twenty-five years old, with a size eight figure and no crow's feet. Why then? Why has my darling husband just dropped the bombshell that he is intending to marry another woman?

'You haven't done anything wrong,' Imran assures me. I notice that his little boy smile fails to reach his eyes. 'I still care for you. Nothing will change.'

Certainly it will. He will be sleeping with another woman for three days out of seven.

'She'll be my second wife and you'll always be my first. This house is yours and I'll rent a flat for her.'

Her? A sob rises in my throat, but I swallow hard. Imran hates tears and tantrums.

'You mean you've already chosen another woman?'

He rakes his hand through his hair, pushing up the brown silk into tufts. At any other time that gesture would have made my heart melt. Not today. Not right now. Not when my whole world is crashing down around me.

'Of course I've already chosen another woman,' he replies, an impatient edge to his voice. 'Why would I bring the drama into our lives if I hadn't already found the one?'

The one. She is the one. There was a time when I had been 'the one'.

'Does she have a name?'

I regret the words instantly. Regret them so much that I want nothing more than for the plush cream carpet that I chose for our new house to swallow me whole. I don't want to know who she is. Knowing will only make this whole nightmare real.

'Husna.' Those big, puppy-like brown eyes soften as her name passes his lips.

I flinch. The spear that has dangled above me since the start of this conversation tears through my heart. He is already infatuated with her. I have already lost him.

He chooses not to notice my devastated reaction. 'She's really nice, and is looking forward to being your co-wife.'

She *wants* to be a second wife? What kind of woman is this? 'She doesn't mind sharing?' I manage in a suffocated voice.

He frowns, the softness evaporating from his eyes as he turns away from me. 'Not all women are selfish like you, Fatima.'

*

I do what all women do in times of uncertainty and strife.

I run to my mum's house. She lives across London on the other side of the Central Line. I fight morning commuters to get my foot in the train and remain squashed between washed and unwashed bodies. Forty-seven minutes later, the open air feels like relief until the freezing cold of January fills my lungs, making me so breathless that I am half bent over when Mum opens the door.

The mad dash to my childhood home has not been worth it, I soon find out. For on hearing my news, Mum, the immaculate housekeeper and much respected community member, sinks into a kitchen chair and covers her face with her hands.

This reaction throws me. 'Mum?'

'Tell me it isn't true,' she sobs, as her heaving shoulders cause her dupatta to slide off her hair, revealing the grey roots.

'Mum!'

She peels her fingers away to shoot a venomous glance at me. 'What have you done? What have you done to push him away?' Her voice rises with every accusation. 'Don't you sleep with him? You have to meet their bodily needs or their eyes wander.'

I can't believe my ears. My mum is finally giving me the sex talk.

'Where has she come from?' Mum demands. 'What does she want?'

I shrug helplessly. 'I don't know who she is or where he met her. I just know that she wants to become his second wife.'

'Stupid woman!' Mum progresses to rant mode. 'Doesn't she realize that if he can do this to his first wife, then he can do it to his second wife too? Does she think there will never be a third or fourth?' She holds up four fingers. 'Four! Islam allows four wives.'

Oh, dear lord. The thought of being a part of Imran's harem makes me want to vomit.

'Listen,' she hisses. 'You must dig your heels in. You can't let him push you away. You can't let the other one win.'

I can't think of anything more undignified than having a catfight over him. Love isn't supposed to be a battle. 'It's not a competition.'

Alarm crosses her face. 'You were first. It counts. You have the advantage.'

Lost for words, I crouch down by the chair, desperate to touch her. My fingers find hers but she snatches them back. It feels like yet another jolt to my heart. Who is this person? What tough love is this? First my husband rejects me and now my own mother! I stand back up.

'Listen to me.' Her eyes fix on mine with renewed determination. 'You will not do anything to dishonour the family. You won't leave him. There will be no divorce.'

Divorce.

The word hits me like a fist to the chest. Saying the word aloud has the same effect on her. Placing a hand on her heart, she murmurs, 'Water.'

I pour a glass at the sink and hand it to her. The water slops over the rim of the glass because her hands are shaking so much. She sips the water before setting it aside. 'Look at me.' She reaches for the hand she rejected minutes ago. I give it, stretching it out to her but refusing to move physically closer to her.

'Promise me you will not divorce.'

'I can't.'

I don't know who is more surprised at these two words, her or me. Only two minutes ago the D word had not even occurred to me, and yet here I am claiming that I can't rule it out.

She struggles to her feet. 'Fatima, divorce means dishonour. It means shame. Don't . . .' She pauses to shoot me an accusing look. 'See what you do to me. My bladder can't take these shocks. I need the loo.'

She leaves me in the stark minimalism of her kitchen. Alone now, the dam bursts and my tears flow. I came here for comfort, but all I've received is talk of dishonour and shame.

My dishonour and shame.

How have my husband's behaviour and actions become my fault?

*

The white walls of the mosque provide sanctuary. It is a Monday afternoon and the women's section is empty. I welcome the silence. I need it as I try to battle the colliding thoughts in my mind. Mum's words repeat themselves again and again.

'Divorce. Dishonour. Divorce. Dishonour. Divorce. Dishonour. Divorce. Dishonour.'

In her attempt to dissuade me from it, she only succeeded in letting the seed grow in my mind.

'Are you all right, sister?'

I glance up at the face marked with concern. The masjid's resident alimah, the title given to a female scholar of the Qur'an, gazes down at me.

'Is it that obvious?' I try to laugh it off, not ready to share my problem with a woman I barely know.

'Well,' she says slowly, carefully choosing her words, 'hardship paves the way to a place of worship. I can see the hurt in your eyes. My sister, you look defeated.'

The acknowledgment of my pain draws tears to my eyes. 'I'm . . .' The sob catches in my throat.

She sits down cross-legged beside me. 'My name's Hawa.'

'Fatima.' I wipe the tears falling freely now with the back of my hand.

'Do you want to talk about it?' she asks gently. 'It sometimes helps.'

What have I to lose?

'My husband wants to marry a second wife.'

She is silent as she absorbs my words and with each passing second I regret my decision to confide in her. Of course she is going to side with Imran! Why wouldn't she? It is her job to reinforce men's privileges.

'And you're not happy with his decision?'

I shift on the floor, reluctant to be fed lines on how I should abide by my husband's wishes. I'm reminded of my mum's words when I left her house. 'You'll be rewarded in heaven for your patience. Allah favours women who obey their husbands.'

I am in no doubt that I want heaven, but not at this price.

'I need to go,' I mumble.

Her hand reaches out to rest on my arm. 'A few minutes, sister. Do not leave this place without finding peace.'

I can't hold back my frustration. 'I don't want you to tell me to suck it up.'

She blinks, the surprise evident in her expression. 'Why do you think I'm going to tell you to,' she pauses, 'suck it up?'

'Aren't you?'

'No.'

'Oh.'

'My sister, may I share a few words about our Prophet Muhammad, peace be upon him?'

I repeat the traditional words of peace under my breath.

'Did you know that he had a twenty-five-year marriage with his first wife Khadija?'

Twenty-five years? 'That long?'

'Do you know much about her?'

I shrug. 'She was a wealthy, successful businesswoman who became the first Muslim.'

Hawa nods. 'Indeed. The Prophet married her when he was twenty-five years old and she was forty. Theirs was a marriage filled with love and respect.'

Everybody knows that. So what? Where is the alimah going with this?

'In our Islamic tradition we are taught to follow the practices of the Prophet. The sunnah. Yes?'

It is my turn to nod.

'We regard him as the best of mankind and aspire to his characteristics of kindness, generosity, compassion – and commitment to women's rights.'

I feel I should say something to demonstrate that I'm not totally ignorant of our Prophet. 'I know he fought against the practice of burying baby girls alive.'

Hawa smiles, looking pleased. 'Yes, he did. But we were talking about his marriage to Khadija. Did you know that he remained faithful to her until her death?'

I shake my head.

'In all those twenty-five years he never took another wife despite it being the custom of the Arabs to have a number of wives. The Prophet loved and cherished Khadija.'

'True love,' I murmur.

'Do you think Muslim men should aspire to the example the Prophet set with his first wife?'

The alimah was asking me for my opinion? 'But I'm sure he had other wives,' I reply. 'My husband says so.'

Hawa agrees. 'He did – but he married again only *after* Khadija's death. And those were either marriages of political alliance or were for the purpose of providing protection to the widows of his companions.'

I gaze at her. 'Why are you telling me all this?'

'Because I and a number of alimah believe that this idea that men are permitted to have four wives needs further reflection. Remember, in early Islam the Muslim men were away at war for months and years. It wasn't about variety. It was about keeping halal relations.'

'Oh.' I did not know that.

'The Qur'an permits men to take more than one wife, but then makes it almost impossible at the same time. The wives must be treated equally in everything: income, wealth, time and love. How is it possible to do that? There can be no favouritism.'

I remember the way Imran's eyes softened when he mentioned my rival's name. Does he have the same look when he talks about me to her? I doubt it. A sharp pain shoots through my chest. Even jealousy is taking a physical form.

'I don't think my husband will listen to your reasoning,' I mumble.

'Perhaps he won't. It is his prerogative. But you don't have to put up with it either.'

I don't understand. 'How can I stop him?'

'You can't. But you don't have to remain his wife either.'

Comprehension finally dawns. She is advising me to break up my marriage. I have been married for three years. Can I just walk away without a fight? Another thought occurs to me. Do I want to fight for him, now that I know he can share his heart so freely with another woman?

My thoughts are interrupted by the muezzin's voice through the speakers. Hawa closes her eyes as she gives herself up to the rhythmic call of the prayer. The first line of the azaan belts into the room.

Allahu Akbar, Allahu Akbar
God is great, God is great.

When it's over, she opens her eyes and smiles. 'You will stay for salat, sister?'

I nod, feeling some of the burden lift off my shoulders. Hawa is a scholar of Islam, learned in the rights of women as dictated by the Qur'an and practised by the Prophet. She has informed me that I will not be committing a sin by leaving my husband.

Without knowing it, she has given me the most valuable gift: the permission to leave my husband without believing that I have compromised my faith.

My mum can stuff her cultural concept of dishonour where the sun doesn't shine.

*

The front door bangs. He is back. The sound of his routine travels up through the stairs: the gym gear lands in the hallway, left for me to pick up, sort and wash. The fridge door creaks and I guess he is gulping juice straight out of the carton, his saliva spreading on the cardboard.

My nose wrinkles in disgust. Islamic etiquette has always been important to me and discovering Imran's Neanderthal ways after our wedding was disappointing to say the least.

I still remember my shock at the revelation that the man I'd married was one of those rare Muslims who refuse to use a bidet in the bathroom. He fell into the wipe and go category. Even my mum noticed. 'Probably thinks it makes him Westernized to have a dirty bum,' she sniffed.

Still for three years I kept quiet, not wanting to rock the boat.

Now I just feel disdain for his habits. Is that what happens when people fall out of love? Do they feel disgust at every little habit?

It has been two weeks since he informed me of his intention to marry another. I've avoided him, pretending to be asleep or hiding in the home office with work as cover. He's left me alone, always busy on the phone. With her. I can't even hate her. I refuse to allow myself to harbour negative feelings for a woman I haven't met. She hasn't broken any promises to me. He has. His vow to be my husband. Always to put me first.

I wait for him now in the bedroom, surrounded by darkness. These days lightbulbs hurt my eyes because of the lack of sleep. I hear him on the stairs and then the door wrenches open. I see the outline of the juice carton in his hand. Sometimes he spills juice on the carpet and when he leaves I get on my hands and knees to scrub the stains out. How have I never resented him for that? There are so many questions now that begin with 'How?'

He is startled by my silhouette on the bed, but recovers fast. A finger flips on the light and the brightness makes me blink.

He doesn't notice my discomfort. 'Why are you sitting in the dark, babe?'

'We need to talk,' I declare, shivering slightly despite the warmth of the central heating.

He cocks his head to the side in the way that I've always loved. Another 'How?' pops up in my head. How had I ever found that dog-eared puppy look appealing before?

My mind fleetingly goes back to the first time. We met on Singlemuslim.com, chatted online for three weeks before arranging to meet at Pret in Liverpool Street station. I'd smiled up at him, inwardly delighted at his six-feet height, broad frame, and that stylish hipster beard. He'd responded by cocking his head, eyes travelling from my Manolo Blahnik heels all the way up to my Burberry trench coat. I had saved all year for my designer wear and these items only came out on days when I needed to impress.

Ah, the naivety of a single girl, making a little money in the City and giving all the wrong impressions. The look had put off 98 per cent of the men that I'd met through the matrimonial website. 'You look high maintenance,' had been their brush-off. They'd scarpered at the idea of a wife whose wardrobe purchases would cost more than the monthly mortgage. Except Imran. He'd cocked his head to appreciate the view, and my toes had curled with glee inside my Manolos. And now? Well, now I struggle to keep the contempt from my face.

He notices. I see it in the way his brow furrows and nostrils flare.

'What's up?' He swigs from the carton.

Now that I have his full attention, I can't find the words. My lips refuse to move.

In an instant he is bored and turns away from me to his side of the wardrobe. 'There are no clean pyjamas in here?'

'I guess not.'

He spins back round, surprised. 'You haven't done my laundry?'

I raise my chin, a small act of defiance. 'No.'

'Why not?' He looks genuinely puzzled.

'I want a divorce.'

My voice lacks conviction and he knows it. That explains the laughter. 'Yeah, okay, but babe, don't take it out on my clothes. What am I supposed to wear?'

That does it. I summon the willpower to confront him. I've never really done it before. It has always been easier to go with the flow and do what he wanted. Not now. Not any more.

'I'm serious.' My legs feel like jelly, but I force myself to stand. 'I want a divorce.'

'Why?'

'What?'

'Why do you want a divorce?' He waves his arms around the room, spraying drops of juice on the carpet. 'You have everything a woman could want.'

He thinks that is enough? A roof and food. 'Marriage isn't about material things.'

'What's it about then?' he demands in exasperation. 'I'm providing for you like a good husband should.'

'You're sharing your love.'

'So damn possessive!' He turns and slams the carton down on my dresser. It is cream in colour, like the carpets, and will now bear a stain. I fight the urge to grab a cleaning cloth and shove it between his hands.

He turns back to me with a determined look. 'A second wife is permitted by the Qur'an.'

'In exceptional circumstances.'

He is taken aback. He didn't expect a response. He wasn't prepared for me to be prepared. 'What are you talking about?' he demands. 'What exceptional circumstances?'

'The Prophet Muhammad (peace be upon him) loved his wife Khadija.'

His mouth tightens, deepening the lines from his nose to his mouth. He considers his answer, one that will shut me up with a knockout blow. 'He had eleven other wives.'

'After Khadija died.'

He blinks. I am not on the floor, bleeding. 'So?'

'So follow his example. Look at their love story and aspire to it.'

His eyes narrow in suspicion. 'Who've you been talking to?'

'No one.'

'Someone's planted these ideas in your head,' he accuses, suddenly grabbing my arm. 'Who?'

His fingers are biting into my flesh. I will have to confess. 'An alimah, if you must know. A learned scholar of Islam who knows what's right and wrong.'

He snorts with disgust, releasing his grip. 'A feminist alimah. Yeah, that's all we need. The Qur'an being reinterpreted to suit modern women's thinking.'

'No,' I say firmly, ignoring the soreness in my arm. 'She has a point. She says to follow the example of the Prophet.'

'Your alimah cannot deny that the Qur'an permits it,' he grinds through clenched teeth.

'Only in exceptional circumstances,' I repeat.

'Yeah, well, my exceptional circumstance is that you are not enough for me.'

I open my mouth to retaliate, but no words emerge. The rage has consumed my ability to communicate. All I can feel is a red haze. I understand now what they mean by crime of passion. A gun. A knife. Either would do right now.

Silence stretches. Eventually I say it again: 'I want a divorce.'

Those puppy eyes turn to slits of ice. He looks ugly and frightening. I keep my chin high up in the air.

'I refuse to divorce you.' He folds his arms across his chest. 'What are you going to do?'

I expected this and am ready. 'You can't bully me. I know about my rights. If you refuse to divorce me then I shall go to a sharia court to ask them to issue one. I don't have to remain married to you if I don't want to.'

First shock and then disbelief. He doesn't know what to do with me. What to say to me. He begins to pace up and down, a tactic to dominate the room. To dominate me. I refuse to move from my spot, to give up my space to him. Finally he comes to a halt to glare at me. 'You want a divorce? Fine. I divorce you. Talaq!'

My stomach somersaults. He just used the Arabic word for divorce. Talaq. I'm nearly there.

'Now get out of my house!'

I draw a deep breath. 'I'm not going to leave without what's mine. We have to divide the assets.'

A slow smile spreads across his face. He reminds me of the Joker in *Batman*. 'What assets? We're not legally married.'

I gawk at him. He's denying the marriage witnessed by hundreds of people. What kind of sociopath have I married? 'I have a copy of our Nikah certificate.'

He shrugs. 'So what?'

His dismissal is making me uneasy. 'So it proves we're married.'

'It does. A halal marriage is what we had.'

'Yes! Halal being the operative word. Not that clued-up after all, eh?' he sneers.

I wait for him to enlighten me. He enjoys my confusion, allowing long seconds to pass. Finally he says, 'The Nikah isn't a legal contract. It means nothing in British courts. According to the law, we've just been living together. You have no claim on my house or my finances.'

The penny finally drops. My name is not on the mortgage. He purchased the house before we married. There is no joint bank account. He told me he would pay for the biggest expense, the mortgage, while I should pay for the household goods. It is my money that has paid for the carpets and sofas, the new kitchen, and the electricity and gas. My money.

'You're l-lying,' I stutter.

Boredom returns. 'Do what you want, Fatima. Just know that you won't get a penny from me.'

I'm on my phone as soon as he walks out. A simple Google search and his words are confirmed. I have no legal rights. How can my father have given me away in marriage without securing my legal rights, my future? Why was a happily-ever-after union assumed so readily? What about the rainy day?

I sink down on the bed and cry and cry until the hiccups start.

If I leave him, I'll have nothing.

If I stay, I'll have to share him with another woman.

The morning sun streams through the gap in the curtains when my decision is finally made. Afterwards, I feel only relief. I don't care about cultural concepts of dishonour. I need to live in peace. I'm twenty-five – I can start again. He can keep the carpet and furniture. My dignity is worth a lot more.

Waiting for the Bus

Sairish Hussain

People are setting fire to their belongings. Furniture, photos, family heirlooms. Ismail can see the flames, but he no longer smells them. His nose is used to the scent of burning now. Burning is normal, it is the most natural thing. On the other side of the road, families cling to each other, crying. They're huddled in their masses, starved, injured, and silhouetted against fallen buildings. The air is putrid, the sky grey with smoke. Homes stand derelict, as do humans.

'The buses are coming.'

Ismail hears this phrase dancing on everybody's lips. *The buses. The buses. The buses.* They're green, these buses, and each can carry around fifty people. Ismail wonders if they also have wings. He hopes they're bulletproof too.

There are solitary figures amongst the crowd. Ismail recognizes a few. There is the baker from whom Ismail always bought his bread. The family doctor who treated all his ailments, from a cold to a broken leg. And Ismail's childhood football coach who oversaw his most carefree days. They are all standing alone, expressionless and covered in soot.

Ismail himself has left the bodies of family members entombed under rubble. He'd rather be there with them. It would be less painful than standing here and waiting for the bus. How blissful it would be to feel nothing at all! Instead, he turns his attention once again to the graffiti on the wall: **DEFIANT UNTIL DEATH**, it reads in red spray paint. He's been staring at the words for a whole hour. It is all he has left. His eyes travel around each curve and swoop of the Arabic script. It might as well be written in blood.

A few yards away from him, Ismail notices a young woman. He knows her name is Razan, as they went to school together. She is also alone, her expression identical to the other defeated faces in the crowd. When Ismail turns to face her, he notices that Razan is holding something. He walks in her direction and sees she is carrying a white helmet.

'I just want to be alone,' Razan says as Ismail reaches her. He hangs back but is desperate to talk to someone. He needs to get out of his own mind.

'Just because you and I are standing together doesn't mean we're not alone,' he says.

Razan clutches the helmet tighter, as Ismail glances back at the graffiti on the wall.

'Is everyone dead?' he asks, matter-of-factly.

Razan nods her head. 'Hmm.'

'Sorry.'

'Are all yours dead too?' she asks.

'Yeah.'

Razan's face is ghostly white and a black hijab is wrapped tightly around her head. A tattered winter coat hangs off her frame which is slender except for the roundness of her belly. Ismail's heart lurches and he quickly averts his eyes.

'We'll be out of Aleppo soon,' he says, by way of consolation.

'I'd rather have died here.'

He looks at the white helmet. 'Who does it belong to?'

Razan's mouth opens, then closes. Ismail can feel the pain radiating from her.

'Sami,' she whispers, without looking up.

'Who is Sami?'

Ignoring him, she asks, 'What about you? You've been staring at the wall for ages.'

Ismail falters; he hadn't thought anyone would notice.

Razan turns to him for the first time and looks him in the eye. 'Do you know who wrote those words?'

'Yes,' replies Ismail.

'Who?'

'Amal. Her name was Amal.'

'Who is Amal?'

'She . . . Somebody I loved.'

'What happened?' They both speak at the same time, hesitant as to who should tell their story first. There is plenty of time to confide in one another, for nobody knows when the green buses will arrive. Although she feigns reluctance, Ismail knows Razan needs to talk to someone too. She is teetering, almost off-balance, almost ready to combust. Ismail sits down on a fallen rock and gestures for her to do the same. She takes a seat too, her movements slow and heavy.

'Shall I start?' Ismail asks.

'No, I'll . . . I'll go first,' Razan stutters, cradling the white helmet against her chest.

*

I wish you didn't have to be the hero, Sami. I wish you hadn't saved all those people, pulled them out of the rubble, reunited brothers and sisters, parents and children. You may think I am selfish to say that, but if you had been selfish too, you would still be here.

You joined the helmets four years ago when you were twenty-one, but you promised me you would leave once we were married. After that, I would be your priority, you said, and our survival would be too. Sami, you lied.

When you'd go out to the headquarters in the morning, my life would hang by a thread. My fingers would tremble as I cooked the evening's dinner, not knowing whether you would ever get to taste it. My stomach would turn whenever I cleaned and dusted around our home, not knowing when or if you would frequent it again. The worst thing was making the bed in the mornings, not knowing if I would ever wake up next to you again.

When I told you this, you'd remind me, 'When I'm out on the job, my mind is here . . . with you. I'm always worrying about you too.'

It became a competition of who was worrying more. You might have been there in the middle of the action, Sami, but I could also hear the airstrikes. For a moment I would stop breathing. Then my imagination would run wild. I could imagine you and the other white helmets sitting together on the ground and sharing flatbread over lunch. I could imagine the food dropping from your mouths and fingers. Your eyes collectively becoming alert. The staggering feet running to the window. The pointing. The shouting. Then would come the explosion.

Equipment would be hastily snatched up. Urgent hands would grab at car keys. The vehicles would follow the smoke and the ash, the obliterated buildings, the screams. Brakes would screech to a halt and, while everyone else ran away, you would run in.

When we'd curl up together in the evenings, the only times we were ever at peace, you'd tell me about the dead and injured bodies. To me, they were nameless and faceless. I couldn't let myself get more involved. But for you, it was different. You and your friends were there, sometimes at the last moments of a person's life. Sometimes just as their souls drifted from their bodies. You'd wrap the remains in bags, carefully, with as much dignity as anyone could muster. You saw their faces and imagined their dreams. What could have been.

'They're like my family,' you'd say.

But I didn't want them to be. I didn't want to share you with anyone else. Sami, how I wish you had cared less.

There were other times, of course, when you'd come bounding into the house and take me in your arms. You'd talk animatedly, your hands moving in quick gestures, your eyes alight. You'd saved people. Mothers. Children. Pulled newborn babies from collapsed buildings. Held them in your arms. On those days, my heart burst with pride and I knew why you had chosen to volunteer. Everything made sense. Hope would dance around in the air between us. Those days were rare though, because look where we are now. You held other people's children, Sami, clutched them against your chest, but you'll never hold your own.

During the summer, you went to Turkey for rescue training. This was never your chosen path, after all, nor was it for any of the other men you worked with. They were builders, tailors, bakers, engineers, teachers. You were once a university student. Barrel bombs put an end to your studies.

For a whole month you were gone while I stayed with family. You left with pen and notebook in hand, eager to learn all you could. Eager to be passionate about something once again. We'd talk on the phone late into the night. For once I didn't worry about you because you told me that there was no war over there. War had ceased, simply by crossing a border. Over there, you could close your eyes and look upwards, and there would be nothing but calm. When you'd open your eyes, birds were flying, not drones. You would notice the wafting clouds, the clear blue sky. Buildings were intact, and so were human beings.

'There's peace,' you'd whisper. I could almost feel your breath on my cheek. I'd cry myself to sleep.

You might have been away from the war physically, but that didn't stop you from worrying about us. After training, you would all retreat into your hotel rooms in groups. The majority of your free time was spent hunched over TV screens and mobile phones that relayed news of the war back home. An airstrike here. A car bomb there. ISIS on the ground. Russia in the air. Men were hanging off every word.

'Even when we are not there, we are there,' you told me.

Your friend, Khaled, lost his brother during an air raid. You comforted him as best you could, then left him to cry alone. The next morning, he put on his uniform and white helmet, and carried on as normal.

I remember how bittersweet it was when you returned. I couldn't wait to be close to you again, but you seemed withdrawn. Sadder.

I came into the room one evening and saw you sitting at the dining table. You were so quiet, I might not even have noticed you. Your eyes were fixed on the TV, more news footage of the war. Your face expressionless. You were gently thumbing your prayer beads.

'Bismillah . . . Bismillah . . . Bismillah . . .' You spoke softly, taking long, mournful breaths between each word.

My grandfather used to do that. Yours probably did too. It was what old people did. They'd sit quietly in corners of the household while children and grandchildren bustled around them. Elderly people with plenty of time to seek comfort in prayer. People who were near the end. I said this to you and you smiled.

'I am old, Razan . . . I am.'

You were killed shortly after we celebrated your twenty-fifth birthday. You were crushed under falling debris – they told me death was instantaneous. You died before the birth of our child. You knew about the baby though. At least you knew.

Sometimes I am so angry with you, Sami. Why did you not keep your promise? Why didn't you abandon this work once we married? If you had, we could have been a family. We could have escaped together on the green buses. You, me and our baby. Because of you, I had to survive the siege alone. I watched the army drag people out into the streets and shoot them in the back of their heads. People I knew starved. Barrel bombs pierced the flesh of my loved ones.

Why could I not have loved you in a different time, in a different country, in a different place altogether? What did we do to deserve this?

People who knew you will always remember you as a hero. I wish you didn't have to be a hero, Sami. I wish you could have just stayed alive.

*

Razan is shivering. Ismail wants to reach out and touch her. Keep her warm. Her arms are wrapped around Sami's helmet, the bulge of her baby bump hidden behind it. Ismail clears his throat, searching for the right words.

'I'm sorry,' he finally says. 'May Allah grant him the highest rank in paradise. He was very brave and –'

'Yes, I know,' Razan interrupts. She's almost bursting at the seams with pain.

'So,' she says, wiping her eyes and turning to Ismail. 'You tell me your story.'

Ismail glances at the crowd before him. There is still a flurry of activity. Belongings continue to be packed or burned. People are still clinging to one another. Children run around in the streets for the first time in weeks. Anxious eyes glance at the clock. *The buses are coming, aren't they?*

What if it is just a ploy? A way of gathering the remaining survivors into one big group. What if there are snipers on the roof? What if bullets are about to rain down on them all? Ismail responds to this thought with no fear or dread. He no longer feels anything.

'Amal,' Razan prompts him. 'You said her name was Amal?'

Ismail nods. He bites his lip, turns to the graffiti on the wall, and begins to speak.

*

Amal, I touched your hand months before I saw your face. It was in the middle of the night and I couldn't sleep. I heard the sound of movement outside and went to the window. A group of people were huddled against a bare wall, paintbrushes and aerosol cans in their hands. I watched the shadows of you working away, mobile phones lighting up different sections of your work. I worried for you all so much that I stayed by the window to keep watch. That's when bullets started firing in the distance. You all scattered in opposite directions, except for one person, who seemed to have just frozen . . . You.

I ran downstairs while my parents slept soundly. Nobody was disturbed or surprised by gunfire any more. I flung open the door. You were crouched on the ground a few yards away, your hands covering your ears. I shouted to get your attention and you made a dash for it, heading in my direction, your hand outstretched. I grabbed it and pulled you inside.

You stayed hunched in the corner of the room, up against the wall, your back towards me. When you had caught your breath, you glanced round at me fearfully. After all, I could have been anyone. You were covered from head to toe in a burqa and though the room was in semi-darkness, I saw your eyes.

Your eyes were enough to draw me in.

'What were you thinking?' I said, trying to focus. 'Do you know how dangerous —'

You tutted and got up, making for the door.

'You can't leave now,' I whispered urgently.

'I need to find my friends,' you said.

'You can find them in the morning. That's if they're not already dead.'

'So, I'm just supposed to stay here all night . . . with you?' you said, pulling your abaya around you.

'I doubt it's the most outrageous thing you've ever done,' I replied, 'having just witnessed you painting graffiti on a wall in the dead of the night.' As everybody in this country knew, that kind of thing led to wars.

I think you smiled at me then. I'm not entirely sure, as your face was half-covered. But I saw those eyes twinkle.

You told me your name was Amal.

'I'm Ismail,' I said. 'What were you writing on the wall?'

You shrugged. 'You'll see it in the morning.'

Then you sat down again on the floor, as far away from me as possible. I stayed on the other side of the room, at a respectable distance.

'And what good do you think it will do?' I enquired.

You got angry again.

'You can take the piss all you want,' you replied. 'We do what we do to remind *them* that we are still here.'

'It'll help no one,' I said.

'It helps me,' you shot back.

I wondered whether I should get you a blanket and leave you alone. It was the modest thing to do, after all. But I couldn't. I wanted to stay and listen to you talk. You told me that you used to be a calligraphy student. When the university was shut down, you became a street artist. You always had the steadiest hand in class.

'That's why I write the words while the others draw the pictures,' you said. 'Sometimes we only have minutes to work.'

It was risky. Your family had no idea that you would sneak out in the middle of the night, but you did it for freedom.

'When I hold a pen or a spray can in my hands, it's the only time in my life I have any power. If there hadn't been a war, I probably would have found a different way to rebel.'

'How?' I asked.

You looked at me and I saw a smirk in your eyes. 'I don't know . . . maybe I would have eloped with a boy.'

Then you asked me about me.

'I'm just a tailor,' I said, suddenly feeling small and pathetic. I realized I had forgotten that power and control was something I could have. It didn't occur to me.

'Nobody is "just" anything,' you said. And that was the moment I became captivated by you.

We talked for a couple of hours before you left at the first sign of dawn. Just as you disappeared, I saw the graffiti you and your friends had drawn. It was of a woman surrounded by the bodies of dead infants. **HAPPY MOTHER'S DAY**, you'd written.

My heart ached for the rest of the day, my mind filled with nothing but thoughts of you. I didn't even know whether you had reached home safely. I thought I would probably never see you again.

But I did, a couple of months later. A loud banging on my door in the middle of the night woke me up. I was gripped by fear. Had they come to take me away? Surely not. I was just a tailor.

That was when you bounded in through the door accompanied by two friends, pleading for a safe place to hide. This time, I was angry.

'You have to stop this, Amal,' I said. 'You're going to get killed.'

'An airstrike will probably kill you in your sleep,' you snapped back. 'I'd rather be doing something for the resistance.'

'Scribbling on a wall is not resisting,' I shouted. 'Please put an end to this.'

You didn't, of course. You and your friends continued. I'd see your graffiti all over the bullet-ridden walls of this city. The flashes of colour, the frenzied portraits of missing people, the defiant slogans. You were right. It did remind everyone that we, the people, were still here. I also saw you. More and more of you. We'd talk on the phone. You'd tell me when you were going to venture out at night with the gang.

'Leave your door open for me, Ismail,' you'd say over the phone.

I'd pace the room, as restless as the flickering lamp in my window. I begged you to let me join you so I could make sure you were safe. You'd hang up the phone whenever I suggested it.

If you got the chance to stop by, you would. You casually removed your face veil a few months after I first met you. It made me love you even more. We created our own bubble away from the war. We'd embrace and kiss and hold each other while rockets rained down and families were obliterated and buildings collapsed.

Then one day, I mentioned marriage. It scared you, I think, because that meant thinking of a future. It scared me too. And that was when I begged you to put away your pens and paint. Graffiti artists had been targeted by snipers. They were being dragged away in the middle of the night by armed men. Taken to torture dungeons. Shot down in the street. I couldn't lose you. You promised me you'd stop, Amal, you promised. But you lied.

Your friend, Hassan, knocked on my door one morning and told me you had disappeared. We looked everywhere, searched every corner of Aleppo for weeks, but no one could find you. That was two months ago and I still don't know what has happened to you. I don't know whether you have been killed or are being held captive. Now, I have been forced to stop looking. If I don't, I will never leave this city.

DEFIANT UNTIL DEATH. That is all I know of your last movements, the last words you wrote on the wall. That is all I have left of you, and now I'm about to leave that behind too.

Sometimes I am so angry with you, Amal. Why did you not keep your promise? Why didn't you abandon this work when I begged you to? If you had, we could have escaped together on the green buses. You, me and our future. Because of you, I had to survive the siege alone.

Me. Just a tailor. But nobody is 'just' anything, you once told me.

Being with you became my resistance.

The sound of growling engines brings Ismail and Razan back to the present. Voices pierce the sky, some clap and yelp, others shout out, praising the Lord. There is a flash of green and from a distance, Ismail can see the buses creeping forward in single file. He stands up but Razan remains seated.

'We need to go,' he says. Razan is looking at Amal's graffiti.

'I can't imagine . . .' she whispers.

'What?'

'How brave she was.'

Ismail turns to face the wall, his heart hurting. 'I'd rather she wasn't brave. I'd rather she was here.'

Razan's fingers grip Sami's helmet. 'Were they better people than us?'

'Maybe . . . but it doesn't mean anything.'

'I don't understand.'

Ismail sighs heavily. He watches as the crowds rush towards the buses.

'Half the people in the city have been vaporized,' he says. 'The world isn't going to remember their names, let alone their sacrifices.'

'We'll remember,' Razan mumbles.

'Life is just meaningless . . .'

'If that's the case, then why don't we just stay here? Let's not get on the bus.' Razan stands up abruptly.

Ismail turns to her, confused. 'What are you saying? We have to.'

'Why?'

'You have to think of your baby.'

'And what do you have to think of? What do you have to live for?'

Ismail does not know what to make of Razan's outburst. 'I . . . er . . .'

'If everything is so worthless and meaningless, why carry on?' she asks him. Her eyes are so challenging that Ismail has to look away.

Those in charge of the buses are ordering everyone to form into groups. Ismail wonders what lies ahead. What trials and tribulations await them all? Everyone is so eager to leave Aleppo, but have people given any thought to the next chapter? The next set of struggles?

Before he knows it, Razan's trembling fingers are wrapped around his. Ismail looks at her, startled. In normal circumstances, he would check to make sure no one was watching. But there are no such things as etiquette and modesty and rules any more. Razan's hand in his hand feels like a blessing. A warmth has spread through his body.

'I need to lay Sami to rest,' she says, her eyes wet. 'Will you help me?'

Ismail nods and lets her lead him. She kneels and places the white helmet at the foot of the wall, directly beneath Amal's final message. She lingers and prays under her breath. Ismail reads and is inspired by the words for one last time: **DEFIANT UNTIL DEATH**.

It is time to walk away. Ismail and Razan join the rest of the survivors queuing up to board the green buses. Their hands are still clasped together.

The Cat That Came
in with the Dark

Sarvat Hasin

There were rules to travelling with her mother, rules that made perfect sense in their world but very little outside of it. First, they could never stay in places numbered 13. In Oxford, they saw six places and the only decent one had the number 13. No matter how much Uzma pleaded, her mother would not relent. It was a gorgeous flat, full of light, but her mother swore it was wrong. 'Something rotten beneath the floorboards,' she insisted.

And so they had to keep on sleeping in a hostel. In the morning, Uzma's books would be spattered with beer from the tourists and students sharing their room. She huddled under the sheets, trying to tuck herself up like an egg roll, uneasy at the sounds of the people around them, their snoring, panting and sleep-talking. Eventually, she and her mother found a small upstairs flat across the road from number 13. By then, number 13 had been broken into. Every morning, as she brushed her teeth, Uzma looked down at the broken windows, shards of glass glittering in the winter sun, and hated that her mother was right about this, like everything else.

Other rules: nothing to tie them to anywhere. No friends back to the house though Uzma could visit theirs. On school forms, she garbled the address. There were cities where they'd had post office boxes but this was not always a given. No permanent attachments. Her mother had a knack for recreating each flat in the image of their first house, like a gauzy dream: scarves over the windows, photographs on the mantelpiece, sticks of incense. But nothing on the walls, not even Blu-Tacked posters, so Uzma had to press pictures of her great loves of stage and screen in between the pages of books, like dried flowers.

They left each place in the same way they found it. Wine stains on carpets preserved, the bathroom's mulch allowed to grow back in the days before they departed. Nothing left behind to show they had been there. It was a practice that Uzma was so used to that she never stopped to think of how tricky this must be, of how her mother's brain must hold all these details at once, a perfect picture of each room.

This new place would be the hardest yet. Clean but barely furnished so when they dumped their bags in the middle of the living room, the flat yawned around them. No wardrobes, just metal rods with canvas flaps holding a mismatch of clothes hangers. None of the usual bones they could hang the trappings of their travelling life over.

When she lay down on the box-spring, the night sounds were louder than they had ever been before, echoing in the empty rooms without the soft cushioning of a home to absorb them.

The cat showed up on a Sunday.

Uzma was finishing her Biology homework in the kitchen. They'd taken down the plastic curtains and her mother was still debating whether or not to replace them. They'd tried to drape a sheet over the window but it never stayed up for long. You'd be halfway through making an omelette and the white sheet would swoop down into the sink like a ghost and have to be dragged out, damp and filthy from the dirty plates piled up there. The sudden flutter of cotton was too much for Uzma and after the second fall, she ripped the sheet off and dumped it in the laundry basket.

It was the middle of November and dark by four. Tonight it was almost seven by the time her mother came home. She'd gone out to get fish and chips but that was hours ago. Uzma put on Mama's favourite music even though she hated the syrupy drone of ghazals. When the key finally scratched in the door, the girl could feel her mouth water in Pavlovian anticipation.

'Sorry sorry,' Mama said. Her arms were full, an oddly shaped bundle piled on top of the chippy bag. 'I made a friend on the way,' she added.

A scarf unravelled on the kitchen table and the cat slunk out of it, only a paw at first and then a tentative ear.

'He ate most of the fish,' Mama explained. 'I'm sorry, bacha, but there's chips for you.'

The carton when Uzma opened it was disappointing: the fat yellow curls of the chips cold and slimy.

'Why do you have a cat?'

'We have a cat. I thought you'd like it – a little friend. I know this place is a bit ghoulish. This one might cheer us up. Come here and meet him.'

Uzma peered into the pile of fur and pashmina, reaching a hand towards it. The shape arched up and away from her.

'Oh dear. Don't mind him.' Mama stroked the animal through the wool. 'He's just a bit shy, I suppose.'

The grey-black arch let out a long, satisfied purr, curling closer to Mama.

'I don't want a cat,' Uzma said.

'Oh, bacha,' Mama soothed, lifting the cat to her face and cooing into its fur. 'You wouldn't turn this little thing out into the cold, would you? He won't be here long – we just need to keep him through the night. It's disgusting out there. I found him curled up on the bridge, shivering in a box of newspapers.'

'It probably belongs to someone. You've just stolen someone's cat.'

'Well, we can let him out in the morning. I'm sure he'll want to go home. And if someone's missing him, they'll put posters up. I bet they'll be glad we looked after him and didn't leave him to freeze in the streets.'

Uzma picked at the chips with a fork. They flopped back into the soggy carton, like dead worms. The cat peeked its head around the pashmina and watched her.

They had been moving this way since she was seven. The longest they'd stayed in one place was a little over a year, in her grandmother's house. All of Uzma's best memories were from there. Nani would make roti and dal, and if Mama was late from work, she would let Uzma roll a roti in butter and sugar and eat it as a snack before dinner. There was a rocking chair in the living room and everything smelled divine but especially Nani, so that when she bent over Uzma every evening to whisper prayers above her head, the whiff of oud calmed the little girl instantly. Even Mama seemed happy, although she and Nani bickered all the time, mostly about Uzma's father, though never directly in front of her.

Everything seemed as if it would go on for ever until one day there was a letter through the door with her father's name on it – and they knew then that he'd found them. They immediately packed up and began moving again.

When they left, Uzma missed her grandmother more than she'd expected. It wasn't clear at the time that this moving around was going to be a permanent state of affairs. Her mother had made it sound as if they were going on an adventure, an extended game of hide and seek from her father. A game whose revelry soon began to fall flat.

*

In the morning, when they put the cat out on the frost-tipped grass, he did not want to leave. He climbed up Mama's trousers, claws digging into her legs. Instead of flinching, she laughed and snatched him up to her chest. 'Don't worry, janu,' she beamed, cupping the cat's face in her palm. 'You don't have to go anywhere just yet if you don't want to. Let's get you some milk.'

From then on, the cat became her shadow. Whenever Mama was in the house, he followed her from room to room. Curled up on the table while she went through the bills for the week, her glasses on the end of her nose, stroking him with one hand. He stayed still when he realized it was necessary, only moving when she got up to fetch a glass of water. Then he'd wriggle himself onto his back and display his soft pink belly. At night, he lay by her bedroom door, yellow eyes unblinking. Uzma had never known an animal to be as self-possessed as this one. All his movements seemed intentional. Her mother thought it was marvellous. She called him Sheba for his regal posturing.

Keeping him was in total violation of all their rules but Mama didn't seem to care. She was lighter now, a tension gone from her body.

'Scientists believe that animals can make your life longer,' she said. 'They reduce stress,' she'd say as he leaped onto her lap immediately after she finished her tea and put the cup down.

Slowly they divided up the flat. It was subtly done but Sheba took over the living room in that first week. There was a single sofa in there, and a round ebony coffee table that they had bought from a charity shop on the outskirts of the city. Sheba rubbed his body on every part of it. Uzma had never seen a living thing take so much pleasure amid so much hostility.

They were eating dinner on the sofa one night, a rare treat that Mama only allowed because she was newly addicted to a series based on a Russian novel and didn't want to miss the final episode. Uzma couldn't really follow it but was easily persuaded by the promise of pizza in front of the television. By the third slice, Sheba had locked eyes with her. He'd climbed onto the needlework cushion Nani had made. There was a Faiz quote on it, Uzma's favourite. Sheba dug his claws into the embroidery and frayed the last few words.

Uzma's territory was the bathroom and her own bedroom. She protected them from Sheba by making sure to close the doors to both rooms before setting off for school. It gave her a secret pleasure to watch the cat get up on his hind legs to scratch at the bathroom door, even if the posture was unsettlingly human.

There was something about Sheba on her bed that she especially hated: rolling around in the sheets, his malicious purring loud as a car engine.

In the early days after they left home, the phone would sometimes ring and there would be no words, just someone breathing down the line. The breathing was their cue to pack up and leave. Uzma thought she could recognize her father from the cadence of his breath but she'd been only a small girl when they had left. There was so little of him she could recall – the cigar breath, bushy eyebrows, fierce black beard, a manner he had of clucking at her with his teeth when he was getting angry.

More than anything, she remembered how it felt when her father was around, that creeping sensation beneath her skin. You'd come home and know immediately if he was there; it had nothing to do with whether the lights were on or off. When he was out, the place was bright and gentle. Soft music, the hiss and sizzle of frying, a pleasant creaking of floorboards. When he was home, the place was a mausoleum. Everything quiet and breathless, as if he'd caught all the air from the house in his mouth.

The phone calls had begun while they were still in Nani's house, several weeks before the letter arrived. It was always Uzma who answered the phone. She never said anything, but it didn't stop her father from talking as if he knew she was there. He spoke with great anger but more patience than he'd had in person. At home, his rages had a great speed to them, as if he couldn't get each word out fast enough. Here, his fury was more measured; he'd pause in between the cursing to plead for her to come home. He never mentioned her mother, only her, the solitary target of his venom.

She wondered if she should have mentioned it the first time he'd called, whether they could have done something to prevent him from coming after them or whether it would have just cut their brief idyll even shorter.

By the time Sheba began sleeping in her mother's bed, Uzma was sick of him. Her mother bought the cat a blanket and his own bowl. She never stopped him from clawing at the sofa. These were disturbing signs that the cat was becoming a permanent fixture in their impermanent life. Whenever Uzma brought up the old rules in protest, they acted out the pantomime again: dropping the cat on the cold grass till he whimpered and climbed up her mother's legs. Then Mama would drag him to her chest to comfort him once more.

These days, she even fed him from her plate, a thing she used to claim was a disgusting practice reserved for white people who thought pets were their children. She let him lick her arm while she did the crossword puzzle, his paws tucked in the crook of her elbow.

In all their years of moving, Uzma and her mother relied only on each other, their own golden bond.

Now the cat was ripping into it with tiny sharp teeth.

The first time they left, it was in the middle of the night. She knew because her mother had told her, and now she could picture it, sneaking out through the door in the dark. Her father passed out in front of the television. Snatches of things, blurry images that she couldn't separate from her dreams. Had she imagined her mother spending nights at the foot of Uzma's bed, a tasbih in one hand, praying softly under her breath?

She remembered knowing that she was the reason they could not stay with her father at home. That her mother had put herself between them until she could not do so any more. When Uzma reached for more than that, the bedroom became a black box.

The door of Uzma's bedroom was open when she got back from school. How had it happened? She mentally retraced her steps that morning: she'd put eyeliner on at the mirror, recovered her headphones from under the duvet . . . Now, something made her flip back the duvet, only to find her bedsheets darkened and damp. Sheba had got in. The cat had somehow found his way into her room and deliberately pissed on her bed.

She rang her grandmother and told her that she thought Sheba was possessed.

'What prayers do you read to get rid of djinns?' she hissed. She was standing in the bathroom with the shower on, so the cat wouldn't hear her.

'Don't be stupid, bacha,' Nani said. 'Djinns don't live in cats.'

Uzma could hear a click and a hiss across the line.

'Are you smoking?'

'Don't be stupid,' Nani repeated. 'And anyway, what do you expect when you call me with these questions? You and your mother are always driving me up the wall.'

'You're the one who said I should call you if I have a bad feeling.'

'A bad feeling, not a stupid feeling. I meant if you see your father outside the house or your mother disappears or someone

90

at school calls you names with murder in their eyes. Not some nonsense about a cat.'

'You're not supposed to be smoking.'

'Ai hai. Don't bother your mother with this. She loves that cat. You don't think she deserves a little affection after all these years?'

So Uzma decided to break a rule too. The prohibition on having friends back to the house was the one she resented the most. After all, it wasn't as if the teenagers she went to school with were likely to be hanging out with a middle-aged Pakistani man.

When she was little, she pretended to be a spy whose location could not be divulged. She made up fantasies of places she could be, Russia or Singapore. But not any longer.

She used to be comfortable in her own company, playing the music her mother hated, making her own food. But Sheba's presence was large and suffocating. She could feel the stony weight of him at the end of the kitchen table while she did her homework, never moving other than the swish of his tail so when she leaned in to get anything she would brush past his whiskers. His fur was bristly and damp, his insistent purring an ugly, rolling sound. The thin white streak down the back of his neck reminded Uzma of her father's head peeking over the sofa, a pale flash of grey hair in the television light. It was awful to be alone with him.

Her mother had brought him into their home without asking her, into the place meant to be only theirs, and so she did not ask either when she invited Daniel over to their flat.

She'd met him at Debate Club. It was the only time in school she felt visibly clever. The debate team wore shiny blue badges.

Mr Martin insisted they wear them every day. He said it would foster a sense of pride in their identity: they weren't just debaters in the classroom, they were debaters everywhere. Uzma, as the newest member, could easily ask for extra coaching.

Daniel's baritone was the reason she liked him. When he stood in front of the podium, it was hard to look away. She practised asking the night before, hoping that in the moment it would float off her tongue as though she'd just thought of it.

Daniel shrugged his shoulders in agreement, ran a hand through his hair as Uzma cautiously tapped her number into his phone. She could feel his pale blue eyes idling over her and resting on her neck, where the skin grew hot beneath the collar.

'Come over whenever,' she said coolly, though later she would text him with more specific instructions, privately having hammered out her mother's schedule to make sure they had a couple of hours in the clear.

It was dark when he got there, the moon pooling in the window, full and bright. She shivered as he took off his shoes by the door. They were alone together. She had never been alone with a boy before. Her carefully constructed lie about a first kiss was that it had happened in a playground when she was fifteen and helping a friend watch his little sister. She'd told it enough times that it was as real to her as a scene from a movie: the midday sun glowing behind her shut eyelids, his fingers tipping her chin and the grass she found later, stuck to her jean pockets in the shape of a cross.

Daniel slipped past the kitchen and straight into her bedroom. He moved with an ease she found impressive. That he would know for sure, without ever having been here before, which bedroom was hers and that it was okay for him to open the door and sit on the edge of her bed. He crossed his legs and smiled up at her.

'Sorry it's so cold in here,' she said. 'My mother thinks heating is bad for the skin. She says if we don't stay hydrated, we'll age faster.'

Daniel laughed and ran a hand through his hair. The sound seemed louder in the house than in class and she could feel something dark twisting inside her in response.

'Your mum,' he said, 'does look very young. I mean, she's pretty hot.'

She could see his eyes drifting over to the photograph on her dresser.

Uzma sniffed and reached for a jumper, shaking the long grey hairs off it. The cat glowered at her from under the desk.

'You have a cat,' he said. 'I love cats.'

'His name is Sheba,' she explained. 'As in, Queen of,' she added, pulling her hair out from the neck of her jumper.

'For a male cat?'

'He's very imperious. And I didn't pick the name. He's not mine, really, just my mum's.'

This seemed to amuse Daniel. He leaned back on her bed. Her hands shook as she flipped open the lid of her laptop. It seemed too intimate to sit next to him so she settled for the desk.

'You live here, so it's your cat too.'

'He's not supposed to be in here.'

'Stop that – you'll hurt his feelings!' Daniel dropped down and reached under the desk. She could feel the warmth of his body through her jeans as he brushed against her. The cat slipped out between her legs, hissing. Crouching down, Daniel smiled up at her. He put his hands on her knees to angle himself out from under her desk, murmuring, 'Sorry,' as he did so. She felt her heart loud in her throat.

When she turned back to face him, Sheba was in the doorway, still hissing, his body arched and ready to spring.

*

Lately, she'd begun to have dreams about her father. In them, he was always standing over her bed as if about to wake her up. It felt hazy but real; remembered.

His heaving breath and still body. His hands stretched out towards her.

They spread the notes out on her bed and pretended to work.

And then she heard the loud, stormy rumbling of his stomach, a growl that tightened her belly. She would have been embarrassed but Daniel only laughed and shook his head, as if gently chastising his body. His hair falling back with his head, its lovely muddy sheen.

'We could order pizza,' he suggested. He stretched across the bed, lazily, reaching for the phone on her bedside table.

'Use yours,' she said.

'Why?'

'I'm not allowed to use the landline.'

'How come?' He lifted himself up to his elbows and peered over at her.

'One of Mama's rules,' she said, and tucked her chin under the neck of her jumper.

Daniel leaned in, so his body hovered just above hers. 'Your mother has a lot of rules,' he said.

'Mmm.'

'Does she cover her head?'

Uzma frowned. 'No. What does that have to do with anything?'

'You said – her rules. I thought that meant maybe she was religious or something.'

'Not those kinds of rules.'

'Oh,' he said, but not as if he understood. 'Rules about boys?'

'We don't talk about boys,' she said. 'Actually, it was always my father who was strict about boys. Even when I was little. When I was four, he got angry when a boy at school gave me a birthday card. It had roses on it, which he took as a sign of his lustful intentions.'

Daniel snorted. 'That's just weird.'

'I suppose so. I don't really remember him that well.'

Daniel's hand ghosted over her ribs, fingers just barely making contact with her jumper. If she took a breath, her body might rise up to meet him.

'But she wouldn't like it that I was here?'

'I guess not.'

He laughed and this time she could feel the sound against her leg. What should she do? Should she pull her arm coquettishly above her head, sprawl back on the sheets? She could lean up to him herself, in case she didn't look inviting enough down here.

He touched her nose. 'You're a bit of a wild child, aren't you?'

She made a noise in her throat, a protest at being infantilized but it didn't come out. Everything stopped when he lowered his mouth to hers. She'd thought there would be a prelude, some sort of build-up to the moment. His chin knocked against hers. At first it was romantic that she couldn't breathe, was pinned to the bed by his weight with the air being sucked out through her lips, but then she began to panic and pushed at his shoulder with her fist. Daniel floated up, disappearing from her grasp as if he was made of air.

'Everything all right?' he asked. He looked so anxious that she kissed him again. This time, she concentrated on what she was doing, touching his hair with her fingers, kissing him instead of simply allowing herself to be kissed. He hooked a hand around her waist and they rolled together. It was a good moment, a very good kiss – until she felt a prick of something dark at her fingers, those not in his hair but curled in the bedsheets. When she pulled free, the back of her hand was spluttering blood. Angry welts were rising in the flesh and Sheba was flouncing off the bed and out of the door.

'Fuck,' Daniel said. 'That looks bad.'

Uzma bit her lip. 'I should clean this,' she said. 'And you should go, maybe.'

Daniel gathered his things and laced up his shoes. Her scratched hand limp on one side, she blinked back ugly tears in the hope he might kiss her goodbye at the door. Instead, he only hoisted his backpack onto one shoulder and slipped out.

Later in bed, she tried to remember everything she could about the kiss. Piecing it back together, moment by moment. How he reached for her, where his hands went on her body. By the end, she had been on top of him, legs around his middle. She tried to remember how they got there. Breathing deeply into the dark, her hand, idle against her belly, snuck down . . .

She remembered: his tongue on her teeth, his chin bristling on her neck, the look on his face when she pulled away, eyes glossy as if he was under a spell. As if she was the spell. He'd touched the small of her back, she remembered now, his fingers under her shirt. If she concentrated on that she could picture it — as if she was watching from above, her own body on this bed with him. It squeezed something tight in her stomach, her breath going soft and high. The wonderfully moist arc of his mouth . . .

The sound of glass shattering snatched her out of her reverie. She sprang up in bed. The shards of a smashed mug lay scattered on the bedroom floor beside her, and Uzma saw Sheba slinking away from the mess, his tail swaying from side to side.

This time, she *knew* she had shut the door.

After that, Uzma stopped sleeping. Coffee before bedtime, no milk. It did not taste good but that didn't matter. She sat up in her bed with a frying pan under the pillow, read murder mysteries to keep herself going. The wounds on the back of her hand had begun to scab over, like purple freckles. She picked at them, each one a reminder of Sheba's claws. If she dozed off her body jerked awake a few minutes later, and she had to endure the jarring sensation of arriving from slumber to a fully lit bedroom. The wakefulness made her sick. She lay in bed, trying not to think too much about Daniel. He hadn't been in school since their kiss, a worrying fact that she tried not to think had something to do with her and his disgust at what had happened between them.

On Thursday, almost a full week into her sleepless vigil, she asked Mr Martin about him.

'We're looking into it, Uzma.' There were spikes of worry in his voice. He didn't tell her, as grown-ups often did, that it was all okay.

On the way home, she hummed to herself under the purple sky. Even in the winter, it was gorgeous to be alone and out of the house. Her ears were cold but she lingered in the streets, dragging her boots slowly as she reached their flat. Inside, it looked warm and yellow. Her mother had promised to cook biryani, a treat to make up for being late back all of the last week, but when Uzma saw Sheba glowering at her through the window she stayed an extra five minutes outside.

'Sit down, bacha,' her mother said when she came in. 'I have to talk to you about something.'

'What's wrong?'

Her mother's hands were shaking around a glass, her rings clattering against it. The biryani smelled burnt, cloves smoking in the pot.

'I'm afraid I've got some bad news. A boy from your school – do you know a Daniel Mayberry?'

'Yes.' She felt an itch in her throat, wondering how they could possibly have been discovered.

'Oh, bacha. Please sit down. Did you know he was missing? Well, they just – they found him last night.'

'What do you mean?'

'His body, I mean. I'm sorry, bacha, I don't have the details for you right now but you should probably sit down and –'

Uzma felt the itch in her throat explode all the way to her brain.

It didn't matter that Mama had no details because they were all over the internet. Pictures of Daniel, his body on the frosty riverbank. The news sites blurred them out but there were others. The crime scene began below his neck, flesh peeled away from the exposed stomach and ribs. She'd touched his chest the other day, the full loud flutter of him beneath her fingertips. Now the live red turned to gunk.

She switched off her phone and dived into bed fully dressed.

'He's not dead, he's not dead,' she said to herself. In the bathroom mirror the next morning, her eyes bloodshot and swollen purple, she said it again, firmly: 'He's not dead.'

From the corner of her eye, she saw the cat slink into the room. He put his paws up on the bathtub behind her and coughed. Sloughing out of his mouth in a ball of fur and hair was a dark blue object. Uzma blinked.

Daniel's Debate Club badge clanged into the bone-white bath like a coin at the bottom of a well.

Rearranged

Noren Haq

'Regrets?' Sapna said as she opened the front door and saw the man standing there. 'I have a few. A few *million*. I was never brave. And when my husband died, everything became clear. I don't remember much of that day,' she went on, as the caller stood, looking bewildered, 'except that all I felt was . . . relief. And then guilt. Huge, choking dollops of guilt that I swallowed with my tea, scalding my throat.'

The man who had just knocked at the front door took an uneasy step backwards. 'Uh, sorry to hear that, hen. But Ah just meant do ye have any regrets wi' yer broadband service?'

'Oh, sorry. Not interested, I'm afraid. But wait, before you go . . .' Sapna reached back into the house '. . . could you open this?' She placed a jar of pickled mango in his hands. 'It's just impossible with my arthritis. I'm making achari pasta. It's – what do you call it? Fusion!' She smiled, happy to have remembered the word.

He returned the unloosened jar, shook his head, and left.

Sapna stood still, embarrassed that she'd shared far too much with a stranger. Again. It was something she felt she no longer had control over. Much like her bladder. 'TMI,' her son would say whenever she happened to mention how she was feeling, physically or emotionally. As if that meant something. Soon real words would be replaced by a universal language of coded initials. Well, one had to keep up with the latest slang if one wanted to stay young at heart.

'Hey, Mrs S!' Her twenty-something next-door neighbour was getting out of his car.

'Hello, Joe beta!' Lovely boy, awful wife.

'Thanks for the shepherd's pie curry. It was amazing.'

'LOL, Joe, I'm glad you liked it.'

Along with her increasingly experimental cooking and vocabulary, there had been many other changes to Sapna's life in the three years following her husband's death. She frequented trendy cafés in Glasgow's West End. Ordered courgette cake and thimblefuls of macchiato from tattooed men in leather waistcoats and sculpted moustaches. She went to New Look and bought jeans. Jeans! But only for wearing around the house. She sang any song that came into her head, her voice gaining in confidence, filling the large empty rooms of her heart. She went to the carnival. Alone. And rode the big scary rides and screamed away her years of sadness and frustration.

Finally, she was free.

Sapna closed the front door and returned to the kitchen to resume her lunch. She opened her laptop and stared at the blank screen. She had wasted her life. She knew it.

She had been married to Gazumpher for over three decades. It had been thirty years of bland indifference. Even on the day she accepted his proposal, she had suspected she would one day find herself telling the story of their engagement with a sigh. But her family wanted her to marry him, and that was the way things were. Not like now, when young people did as they pleased.

She sighed and waited for her laptop to snap into life. She brought up the website, took a bite from her cheese and chaat masala sandwich and typed in her login details.

Username: **58jaffacakes**
Password: **theroadnottaken**

And what had her parents based their decision on? Did they admire his wit? Were they impressed with his charisma? Or recognize the traits of a kind, caring, selfless nature? No. He had the right job. Was the right colour. Sported the appropriate amount of facial hair. She was stabbing at the keyboard, and had to force herself to stop and breathe out her frustration. Well, now there was no one left to disapprove. She typed out the words, Yes. Let's meet. And clicked Send.

*

It was the day before The Day. The day when she would meet the man from the website. And her sister-in-law had come over, unannounced as usual. Sapna knew Pinky envied her the house – Pinky's late brother's house. All that space. The four bathrooms.

Today she'd taken it upon herself to rearrange Sapna's kitchen. Her head was firmly in the fridge. 'Do you know your imli has gone mouldy?'

'I really don't think it's necessary to tidy the fridge, Pinky.'

The head emerged. 'Not necessary? Your masala jars were a mess, and look,' she swung her bulk around the door of the fridge, 'you bought the wrong mangoes – again!' She wrinkled her forehead at Sapna as she waved two mangoes at her, one in each hand.

The multi-coloured tinsel tassels decorating the pointy ends of the fruit gave Pinky the vague semblance of a Pakistani hula dancer. Laughter bubbling in her throat, Sapna hurried to the sink for a glass of water.

The doorbell rang and Pinky went to answer it, still clutching the mangoes. When she came back, she grunted, 'That old duffer, Ahmed, is here to do your windows. He's grinning like an idiot.'

He was on the outside looking in. And that was the way it was. A daydreamer and an underachiever was how people had labelled Ahmed in his youth. Now there was no one to care that he lived with his head in the clouds.

He positioned his ladder and started his ascent. Beautiful house, beautiful windows, beautiful . . . He wiped away the droplets obscuring his view inside. He had spent the last few years imagining he was wiping away her tears, her hidden sadness. He would dream of her. Her face in the dappled light, smiling, happy.

Then he would wake and say, 'Today. Today's The Day.'

But it didn't matter how high he climbed. She was out of his reach.

'Here, Akhmed! Gonny get yer backside down here?' shouted up one of Sapna's neighbours. 'My windows are filthy!'

Ahmed slowly descended, his joints creaking.

Pinky finally left. Mint and apple chilli chicken: Sapna cooked to calm her nerves. The apple rotated in her hand as she peeled and tried not to think of her previous disasters. She'd only started this thing out of curiosity. She wasn't seriously thinking of remarrying at her age. It had all just been to see . . . was there anyone out there like her? In the year that followed, she'd found the answer was no.

It had started out so well. She struck gold the very first time. Or so she thought. SonaSona was clean and interesting and funny. He was a solicitor. He dressed well. And he seemed to like her.

Then, the unthinkable had happened. She dropped her knife and covered her face with her hands as she recalled the excruciating embarrassment.

It was just a simple errand. She was in a hurry that day and hadn't had time to change out of her lounging-around-the-house jeans. She was only running into the supermarket for one essential item. The fact was, she needed more pantyliners to keep her feeling fresh for the day ahead. To give her another level of confidence. To soak up the humiliating result of that weak and ignoble traitor, her pelvic floor.

Sapna had marched straight to the appropriate aisle to wade through the sea of products, and soon popped a box of her preferred brand into her basket. Then she froze in horror as she heard a familiar clopping of heels and a voice that no one could mistake.

Pinky was not far behind her, chatting on her mobile phone.

Sapna ran towards the checkout. The aisles flew past but still she heard the heels, the voice approaching. She could do this.

She could get out unseen, if only she could reach that distant checkout. If only this insufferable man wasn't blocking her way!

That was when she had recognized who was in front of her. SonaSona. Oh God, no!

His back was turned. She had to get rid of the sole item in her basket. She picked it up and hurled it into the adjoining aisle. Then Sapna turned to the shelf next to her and dropped something – anything – into her basket.

In that second she realized her prospective rishta was about to turn around. That's when she heard a light thud and a high-pitched cry.

'Hai, meri Rabb!' Pinky exclaimed. 'Somebody just tried to kill me with a TENA box!'

SonaSona turned around to Sapna. He took in the straggly hair escaping her hijab, her jeans–kameez combo, and smiled. 'JaffaCakes! So nice to see –' He stuttered and stopped talking as though someone had pressed an off switch on his back. He was staring at the item that Sapna had grabbed for her basket and his mouth made a wide O.

She looked, and saw only two words. *Ribbed*. *Flavoured*. Sapna screamed and ran. Only to find she was still clutching her basket as the alarms at the exit began beeping.

She never saw SonaSona again. He never even gave her the chance to explain. Blocked and deleted. All that glitters . . .

And then, against her better judgement, she had agreed to meet up with PunjabiPrinceCharming.

He turned up in a white shalwar kameez, covered in yellow curry stain splashes and sporting a grey suit jacket on top. Every maddening sip of his tea seemed to slurp on into infinity and end with a hideous *ahhhh*! It made her want to lunge across the table and strangle him with her napkin.

Sapna had understood that names matter after meeting HeroNumberOne. The only heroic thing about him was his relentless attempts to suppress his huge gastric burps.

He spoke of nothing but cars. 'Did you know that the turbos in a Mercedes are in the hot V position on the engine?' He pointed his dessert fork at the window, gesturing to his car outside. 'I can show you mine if you like.'

She stared at him, desperately hoping this wasn't his freaky version of an indecent proposal.

And then she had found *him*. In fact, he had found her: he was the one who clicked on her profile.

NotADoctor: Tell me something true . . . something meaningful, beyond the banalities of our profiles. We like reading, we like writing, you like cooking, I like cycling.

58JaffaCakes: Your profile says you like poetry, but it doesn't say you yourself are a poet.

NotADoctor: Hardly! For that I'd need to borrow from the greats. How about this, then: why don't we tell each other real, important things through poetry?

58JaffaCakes: Hmm, not sure. You go first.

And so began their conversation in poetry.

NotADoctor: 'I am – yet what I am none cares or knows. My friends forsake me like a memory lost; I am the self-consumer of my woes.' John Clare.

58JaffaCakes: 'She dwelt among the untrodden ways, beside the springs of Dove. A Maid whom there were none to praise, and very few to love.' Wordsworth.

NotADoctor: 'The caged bird sings with a fearful trill of things unknown but longed for still, and his tune is heard on the distant hill, for the caged bird sings of freedom.' Maya Angelou.

58JaffaCakes: 'Youth is full of sport, age's breath is short; youth is nimble, age is lame: youth is hot and bold, age is weak and cold, youth is wild and age is tame.' Shakespeare.

NotADoctor: 'Their hearts have not grown old.' Yeats.

*

The next day, the day of The Day, and someone was hammering at the door at 7 a.m.

'As-salaamu alaykum, Pinky. Come in.'

But Pinky had already reached the kitchen, removing her oversized sunglasses in a sweeping gesture. She seized Sapna by the wrists and brought her in for an almighty hug. 'Hai, Zumfo bhai has left us! Left us all alone in this world!'

Sapna squirmed slightly, but there was no escaping Pinky. This happened from time to time and Sapna knew what was coming next.

'It's not right, both of us living alone. Zumfo would not have wanted that.' She stepped back, still holding Sapna in her death grip, and stared into her eyes. 'You know, if I lived here, I could make fresh, fresh khana every day. I could get this house in order. You wouldn't have to be alone.'

Sapna smiled. 'Let's have breakfast, Pinky.' She was finally going to meet NotADoctor at noon. She looked up at the clock and wondered how on earth she was going to escape in time.

'As soon as we're done with breakfast, I'm going to start cooking lunch!'

'But there's chicken in the fridge from yesterday,' Sapna told her.

'Bassy khana?' Pinky wrinkled her nose, 'No, no. I'll make something fresh. Then we can go out shopping, spend the whole day together.'

'Actually Pinky, I'm not feeling very well.'

'Heh? What's wrong with you?'

'I . . . I think I'm going to throw up.' Sapna raced to the toilet, hand over her mouth.

'You see what happens when you don't eat fresh!' Pinky shouted after her.

Sapna locked herself in the small downstairs lavatory and collapsed against the door. She did feel sick. Her eyes scanned the room: shiny tiles, large window. Now she knew what to do. She ran upstairs, yelling as she went, 'Need to shower, Pinky! I'm a mess!'

Sapna showered in the en suite and dressed carefully, before grabbing her handbag and creeping downstairs. She heard the sizzling of onions and Pinky bustling about in the kitchen.

'Sapna! Come help me!'

'Sorry, Pinky, it's the other end now . . . *Oww* . . . I think I might be in the bathroom for a long time.' She locked herself in the toilet again.

'Ya Allah, open a window!'

Sapna stifled a giggle. 'Don't worry, Pinky, I will.' She opened the window as wide as it would go. It was definitely big enough. Then she watched it slam shut. She'd been meaning to have that fixed.

Looking around for something to keep it open, she grabbed the lota, wedging it into the far corner. Perfect. She climbed up onto the cistern and threw her handbag outside. She winced at the clattering sound it made. At least the toilet was on the ground floor.

Then she hitched up her kameez and put one leg through, holding the top of the window frame. The glass sparkled in the sunlight, and for the first time she noticed how clean Ahmed kept the windows. She swung the other leg out beside her and tried to shuffle out of the opening and onto the ground below.

She was still holding on tightly to the top of the window frame, her bottom suspended outside, when she found her hips were stuck. Panic gripped her heart. This was ridiculous. What was she supposed to do now? She needed some kind of lubricant to free herself. The sides of the window dug painfully into her flesh. *If only I had some ghee.* And then she remembered her bag.

'Mrs Shah?' The voice to the side of her made her heart jump.

'Who's that?'

'It's me – Joe.'

Sapna felt relieved. 'Oh, Joe. Can you help me, beta? I seem to be stuck.'

'Yes, I can see that,' Joe laughed. 'Shall I call the fire brigade?'

'No! No need for that. Just pick up my handbag,' she implored. 'It should be there at your feet.'

'Wow, it's heavy. What do you have in here, Mrs S?'

'There should be a jar of mango pickle. Take it out.'

'Um. Right, although I think maybe now isn't the best time for a snack . . .'

'Just open it and give the edges of the window a grease,' she said urgently. 'That should do it.'

He shrugged. 'Mrs. Shah, I really don't think —'

'*Please*, Joe.' She heard sounds of straining.

'The lid won't open.'

'Stupid jar! Oh, my leg!' She grimaced. 'It's cramping up.'

'Right, look — let me just try pulling you out instead.'

'All right,' she agreed, 'but be careful, Joe.'

He managed to get his arms around her shoulders.

Oh my God, she thought. If I land on him, I'll break him!

'One.'

Then he'll die!

'Two.'

And his terrible wife will kill me!

'Three!'

With gritted teeth he pulled and they both went flying backwards. There was a crash and the sound of the window slamming shut, followed by silence as they lay sprawled on the ground.

'You okay, Joe?' Sapna panted.

'Still in one piece.' He got up, patting down his trousers, and helped Sapna up. 'Here's your . . . um . . . jug,' he said, passing her the lota.

'Thanks. You must be wondering why I was . . .'

'Making a break for it?'

'Yes. Actually, could you give me a lift somewhere? I'll explain on the way.'

*

Joe parked outside the café.

Her hand shook slightly as Sapna waved him off. She turned, approaching the door. Then she stopped and stared at her reflection in the café window. The face looked pale, wrinkled by time and disappointment. Large and wide, the eyes stared back at her, suddenly full of doubts. She clenched her fists, took a deep breath, and pushed the door firmly open.

He was seated, flicking a plastic stirrer against the table. The windows had steamed up, blocking his view outside. The bell at the door tinkled loudly as it swung open. He turned sharply. The humming bustle of the café seemed to mute as he watched her enter.

Her eyes darted around the queuing patrons, the seated crowd, and rested on him. She approached slowly. 'Ahmed?'

'Yes.' He looked down, unable to meet her disbelieving stare.

'It's you! You're NotADoctor? And you knew it was me, from the start?' she asked.

'Yes,' he admitted.

She sat down in the empty chair, speechless.

'I'm sorry. So sorry, Sapna. I wanted to tell you . . .'

'I can't believe you –'

'I know! I know.' He raked his hand through his hair, eyes closed, trying to find the words. 'I was scared. I'm not brave like you are. I thought if you knew it was me – well, that you wouldn't want . . . *me*.'

His lip trembled slightly and Sapna's face softened.

Ahmed raised his head. There was a dark, burning look in his eyes that startled her.

'Doubt thou the stars are fire;
  Doubt that the sun doth move;
Doubt truth to be a liar;
  But never doubt I . . .'

She held her breath.

He gently placed a small object on the table between them.

And she smiled, and cried, and smiled, her hands to her face. Then Sapna reached into her cavernous handbag for a tissue, emptying its contents onto the table in her search. She wiped her eyes and had begun returning the items when she sat up straight and stared at Ahmed.

He had the jar of mango pickle in his hands and took off the lid with a single quick twist.

Sapna's eyes danced as she reached out, picked up the ring and slipped it onto her finger.

Peter Pochmann
Goes to Dinner

Bina Shah

When Mohammed invited Peter Pochmann to dinner at his house, Pochmann hesitated before accepting the invitation, a humble one-line email slipped in between the daily reports that Mohammed sent him on the progress of their latest project.

'My wife and I would be honoured to welcome you for dinner on Friday evening.'

Pochmann didn't like to play favourites among his employees. If he said yes, he might have to commit the next twenty weekends to visiting one small house after another in Northwood, Harrow-on-the-Hill and even – he shuddered – Pinner.

But then he recalled that Mohammed had recently got married to a woman from Karachi, and Pochmann felt, with a vaguely old-fashioned sense of propriety, that it would be rude to refuse the invitation.

Pochmann oversaw the small Watford branch of a large tech company. Most of the employees – programmers, systems analysts, administrative assistants who kept the company running smoothly – were Asian, a few from Eastern Europe. He was the only Englishman in the office. Despite his lifelong policy of maintaining a respectful distance between himself and his employees, he wanted, somehow, to be *cooler*, more accepted – more multicultural. In these days of Brexit, when Britain seemed to be shrinking, Pochmann wanted to expand his horizons. So he said yes to Mohammed, and made a mental note *not* to bring a bottle of wine on Friday evening.

That Friday, when Pochmann alighted from his car at 24 Gatehill Road, Mohammed was already waiting for him in front of the house. Almost before Pochmann could speak, Mohammed bustled him up the steps to the front door of the small semi-detached house, one of two dozen that lined both sides of the quiet street. Pochmann caught sight of a small garden with a rockery in the corner and, almost as fleetingly, a head-scarfed woman in the upstairs window who disappeared as he glanced up at her.

He blinked in the dim light that illuminated the front hallway. A prolonged wailing was coming from deep inside one of the rooms, and he was immediately able to identify it as the Islamic call to prayer. On a trip to Istanbul years ago, he'd heard the harsh cacophony of the mosques calling the faithful five times a day. Pochmann had been woken every morning before dawn by this chorus. As he lay awake in bed, feeling resentful, he had imagined a man falling from the top of a minaret, howling as he flew through the air to the ground.

But in the half light of this English summer evening, the plaintive crooning made him stop in his tracks and draw in his breath. Night fell abruptly in Istanbul summers, a cool velvet curtain made of indigo that tumbled down upon the stiflingly hot day. Here in England, twilight stretched on for ever: safe, predictable, boring. This man's voice calling out for God made Pochmann long for Istanbul again.

An old man was coming towards him, a pocket-sized version of Mohammed with a close-trimmed white beard and bright brown eyes rimmed cholesterol blue, like Saturn's rings. 'Welcome, welcome,' he said.

Mohammed put an arm around the old man's shoulders. His voice rang with pride as he made the introductions: 'This is my boss, Abba-ji, Mr Peter Pochmann. Mr Pochmann, my father, Mohammed Hassan.'

Pochmann held out his hand and was rewarded with a firm handshake and Mohammed Senior's warm smile. The older man had a beard but no moustache, which made Pochmann do a double-take as he boomed out his standard polite greeting: 'Thank you. You have a lovely house,' and then, as an afterthought, he added: 'sir.' Already this house was making him behave strangely, he thought to himself.

He glanced around the hallway, waiting for Mohammed Junior's wife to make her appearance; he smelled warm spices emanating from the kitchen and hoped that she wouldn't absent herself for the entire evening. The women in his office were noisily visible and confident: speaking in normal English accents, going to the cinema or socializing at weekends. He was curious about this woman, who came from so far away. What would she make of this place, this country – of him?

As if reading Pochmann's mind, Mohammed Senior said, 'Let us sit in the drawing room. Rabeea is preparing dinner; it will be ready shortly.' He ushered them into a small front room, overfilled with puffy sofas, a dining table and four chairs, and dominated by a giant television against one wall, silently broadcasting what looked like a Pakistani news show. Pochmann searched the other walls for family photographs, but there were only some framed prints of Arabic calligraphy, and in one corner, a tapestry depicting the black cube – the Kaaba – from the Grand Mosque in Mecca. A vase filled with tuberoses and gladioli rested on a low wooden table, and Pochmann was made to sit in front of it. He sneezed explosively twice.

'Do you need a glass of water?' asked Mohammed Junior.

'Get him a tissue,' instructed Mohammed Senior.

'I'm fine, I'm fine. Thank you. Just a little hay fever. Flowers, you know.'

'It is allergies,' nodded Mohammed Senior. 'Everyone has them here.'

'My father, in his retirement, has become a qualified herbal doctor,' explained Mohammed. Pochmann thought he heard the slightest hesitation in Mohammed's voice. 'He specializes in allergic asthma.'

'Really?' Pochmann had met enough English hippies to be suspicious of their nonsense, but this sounded slightly more legitimate. 'What does a herbal doctor do? Is it like Chinese medicine?'

Mohammed Senior steepled his fingers together, his face livening up as he explained his methods. 'Oh no, Mr Pochmann, it is much superior to Chinese medicine, or Western. Not only do I use our own herbs – we call it *jarri booti* in Urdu – but also prayers. It is a combination of reading the religious texts and matching the appropriate one to the illness of the patient. Then

116

I make tonics and pills out of herbs that have been mentioned in the Qur'an. It is a very precise science, I assure you.'

'Oh, I see.'

'Yes. It is an elaborate system of Islamic healing, passed down since the time of the Prophet, peace be upon him. Much better than any doctor I have ever encountered in this country.'

Mohammed Junior added a word of explanation or translation here and there, but his expression was unreadable. If anything, he looked slightly embarrassed. Or was Pochmann imagining that Mohammed's lips were pursed as if to prevent himself from interrupting, his anxious eyes glancing at his face to see what effect his father's words were having on his boss?

'And of course, He is the greatest healer.' Mohammed Senior pointed upwards at the ceiling. Smarting at the implied insult to the NHS, Pochmann raised his eyes, wondering if a surgeon lived upstairs. 'Indeed, Allah is the one to grant health or take it away. To give life, or take it away. To Him we belong and to Him we must return.'

Mohammed Senior unsteepled his fingers and sat back, satisfied. 'Beta, go and ask Rabeea how much longer it will take for dinner,' he said. 'Mr Pochmann must be hungry.'

Pochmann longed to ask Mohammed Senior how prayer and herbs would help if someone got into an accident and had to have their legs amputated. But it was important to be respectful of others' beliefs. Besides, he could not have it going around the office that he was a bigot – or an Islamophobe. These were tense times; patience and understanding would get him further than aggressive rationality. Pochmann decided to exercise his English largesse and smile, but only with his mouth. 'It all smells wonderful. I can't wait to try everything.'

'My daughter-in-law is preparing the meal. I lost my wife five years ago, and . . .' Mohammed Senior sighed and looked down at the floor. 'I was not able to eat anything for almost a year. I lost a tremendous amount of weight. The doctors did not know what was wrong with me. So I started researching Eastern medicine. I read all sorts of textbooks on Chinese medicine, Ayurvedic medicine from India, South American traditions. It was only when I turned to the Qur'an for healing that I began to feel like eating again. And when Rabeea married my son and moved here, she helped me even more. She cooked anything and everything that I wanted, no matter how strange it sounded. Because of her love for me, I became better. She is my daughter-in-law, but despite all her flaws – and they are many, many, *many* – she is more like a daughter, Mr Pochmann.' His eyes, warm and tender in the deep hollows of his face, met Pochmann's. 'Do you have a daughter, Mr Pochmann? Daughters are Allah's greatest blessing.'

Despite his alarm at the repetition of the word *many*, for some reason this touched Pochmann. He couldn't help his eyes welling up again, this time not from allergies. 'Please, call me Peter.'

Just then Mohammed Junior came into the room, followed by a woman carrying a dish of food. Pochmann stood up and cast his smile in her direction but froze halfway when he saw that the woman not only wore a scarf on her head, but a cloth pinned all the way around her face. Only her eyes were visible, two dark coals that glimmered in the thin oasis of skin between covered forehead and covered nose.

Mohammed stood up too and shifted his weight from one foot to the other, rubbing his hands together. 'Mr Pochmann, this is my wife Rabeea.' His eyes darted from Pochmann's face to Rabeea's, and back to Pochmann's again. Pochmann felt an unexpected trickle of sweat on his back. Who was this masked woman, and how the hell was he supposed to make conversation with her for an entire evening? Mohammed should have warned him about this! Politeness demanded a simple *nota bene* to his email invitation: 'By the way, my wife wears a niqab. Don't be surprised.'

There was no way to tell what age she was: she could have been fourteen or forty. She wore a light grey housecoat that fell all around her, obscuring her figure. Her hands though, were small and birdlike, the nails short and unpolished. Pochmann glanced at them but kept his own hands behind his back. However, she made no move to indicate that she wanted him to shake hands with her.

'Good evening, Mr Pochmann.' The woman's voice was steady, if a little muffled, her words well enunciated, but from beneath the veil his name came out sounding like *Porkmann*.

'Uh, lovely to meet you – but it's Pochmann, not Porkmann.'

'Is it?' Rabeea turned to Mohammed. 'You said it was Porkmann.'

'No, I didn't.' Mohammed shook his head rapidly, half turning in apology to Pochmann. 'You must have misheard me.'

'Well,' said Rabeea, setting down the dish on the table with a loud clatter, 'thank God for that. I don't like some of these English names. Porkmann. Hamm. Bacon. When I see names like that in books, I shudder. I'm sorry, but I can't help it.'

Mohammed shot off a stream of rapid Urdu in Rabeea's direction. Pochmann had never heard Mohammed speak Urdu before, but the words needed no translation. His wife shot a volley back, the double of Mohammed's in both firepower and velocity. Mohammed shrank, visibly cowed. Rabeea strode out of the room back to the kitchen, while Mohammed Senior, still seated, played with the beads on his rosary and gazed at the TV, where one news anchor had risen from his seat to beat the other one about the face with a microphone.

Pochmann allowed a thought to bubble up to the surface of his mind: Rabeea was a terrorist. At the same time, he realized that her husband was the only person she seemed to have terrorized – with exceptional skill. ISIS could probably learn a thing or two from her.

'I'm sorry,' said Mohammed. 'I should have said something. Rabeea is . . . very devout.'

Pochmann nodded. 'Ah.' He could have said more, but sagacity and silence were often one and the same.

'Yes, but sometimes I think too devout,' Mohammed whispered.

Mohammed Senior spoke up. 'There is no such thing as too much faith!' But even he bit his lip as Rabeea barged into the room again, carrying a large, heavy tray from which she unpacked a series of food-laden platters, a straw basket, and a jug filled with water.

The men watched her in furtive, frightened silence as she set the plates and platters on the table in an artful arrangement. Pochmann noted that neither her husband nor her father-in-law got up to help her. She barely acknowledged any of them; her eyes remained fixed on the food. But she pointedly ignored Pochmann in a way that told him he was the sole focus of her attention.

'Please, the dinner is ready,' she said, standing at the head of the table and bristling, porcupine-like, her hands momentarily waving the men to their chairs before they returned to a tight jailer's clasp behind her back.

Mohammeds Senior and Junior sat down together first. Rabeea stood until Pochmann realized that she would remain standing until he took his seat. He fitted himself into his chair, folding his legs under the table, and watched as Rabeea heaped his plate with a dizzying array of food: spiced meat, fragrant buttered rice, warm flat bread, colourful vegetables. Rabeea did not sit down, even when her husband and father-in-law began to eat. Pochmann had no idea what to do.

'Please, start,' said Mohammed Senior.

'But . . .'

'Yes, please,' said Mohammed Junior.

'What about . . .'

'Please, don't worry about me,' said Rabeea. 'I've already eaten. I am not hungry.'

Pochmann, bewildered, picked up his silverware and spooned a mouthful cautiously between his lips, expecting to either choke or his mouth to be set on fire, as usually happened to him in Indian restaurants. To his surprise, it was delicious. The food transferred itself quickly and pleasantly from his mouth to his stomach, and even before he was done, he wanted more. Rabeea hovered around the table, serving her father-in-law, bringing in more chapatis from the kitchen.

The conversation was relaxed – if a little strained. They stayed away from difficult subjects, his hosts enquiring whether Pochmann liked Pakistani food ('Chicken tikka masala is our national dish,' Pochmann responded, correctly), the English weather, the football.

Once Rabeea had served dessert, a jelly trifle dotted with custard, decimated sponge cake and pieces of cut-up fruit, she sat down at the table with them, sipping delicately from a cup of green tea. She accomplished this by lifting the face veil slightly, inserting the cup underneath, and angling her chin towards the hidden vessel as if she were a pelican dipping its beak into the sea. Pochmann smiled at her, feeling he could even get used to sitting across the table from a woman whose face was covered. He could just think of her as wearing a surgeon's mask.

'So, ah, Mrs Mohammed, tell me, is this your first time in Britain?'

'Yes. It is an expansive trip. Also, it is very difficult for Pakistanis to get a visa.'

Her accent was strange, but he was already getting used to it. It wasn't the cool hybrid of the English accent married with the local Asian one; more of a lilt with a few hiccups here and there, words pronounced in ways he hadn't known the English language was capable of accommodating.

'A lot of people try to cheat and come to this country from the backside. So the people in the High Commission think we are bad people when they see us at the visa counters. Do you think we are bad people, Mr Pochmann?'

Pochmann felt the blow right in the solar plexus; the air flew out of him with an audible whistle.

'Of course not! I don't think that at all. Pakistanis are fine people, from what I've seen.'

'And what have you seen, Mr Pochmann?' She tilted her head to one side, staring at him. She had the longest eyelashes he'd ever seen on a woman, so long that when she blinked, they swept up and touched her thick, bushy eyebrows. He found himself irritated that he couldn't see her face, couldn't tell if the question was innocent, cynical or flirtatious. And, maddeningly, he found himself wondering about the rest of her body: was she slim or rounded, large-breasted or flat-chested? Did she have pronounced hips or a board-like physique?

'Well. Ah. From what I've seen so far, Pakistanis and the English aren't so very different.'

'Oh, really?' Mohammed Senior's face lit up again. 'In what way?'

Rabeea narrowed her eyes. 'Yes, in what way?'

Now he'd have to come up with something. 'Well, we all . . . ah . . . love our families! Family is important to all of us. It's universal.' He nodded happily.

'But isn't it true that the English throw their children out of the house when they reach eighteen, and put their parents in nursing homes?' Rabeea arched an eyebrow, managing to convey both disbelief and triumph in the slight lift. 'How can you say you care about family?'

'That's a terrible generalization. It's not true at all.'

'Where is *your* mother?'

'Dead,' said Pochmann quickly.

Rabeea didn't miss a beat. 'And your father?'

'Also dead.'

'You're an orphan?'

'Yes.'

'Who looked after you? Your uncles, aunts? Grandparents?'

'Nobody. I was in care, and then I was adopted by my foster parents. They were the most amazing couple, they were so wonderful to me . . .'

'But that's terrible!' Now both of Rabeea's eyebrows were raised high, caterpillars rippling duskily across her forehead. 'Nobody to take care of you – your relatives just abandoned you! That would never happen back home. We love our children. More than our own lives.'

Something about the tone of Rabeea's voice – the smugness, the certainty about a place she couldn't possibly know, having only just arrived – infuriated Pochmann.

'Is that why so many girls are forced into marriages with their cousins *back home*?'

Mohammed turned his face to Pochmann, his eyes pleading. Rabeea's face betrayed nothing – it couldn't – but Pochmann could feel her anger turning towards him with the same sort of cold, blind hunger that lionesses use to stalk their prey.

'It is not true. That is just negative propaganda to make us look bad. There is no such thing as forced marriage!'

'Then why . . .'

'It is not allowed in Islam. A woman must give consent to her marriage. I did. I was not forced to marry *him*, even though he is my cousin.' She nodded contemptuously towards Mohammed, who managed to look grateful at the unspoken insult.

Shit, thought Pochmann desperately to himself.

'Have you read the Qur'an, Mr Pochmann?'

'No, I have not,' he said defiantly. Even though he felt as though he had swum into deep waters and could no longer feel the ground under his feet, he refused to feel ashamed for his ignorance.

'You must. It is the only way to understand how we feel.'

Pochmann wanted, for a brief moment, to smack her. This was a Christian country: *she* should be reading the *Bible*! How would she react if he demanded that she read the Bible, quizzed her on biblical verses and asked her why her religion taught people to blow themselves up in the name of God? He pushed away his plate. The sweet jelly and custard, which had just a moment ago tasted so good, was now broken glass and sand in his mouth.

'Have some more.' Mohammed leaped from his seat and brought the serving dish towards Pochmann. 'Please!'

'I've had plenty, thank you.'

Rabeea started to clear away empty dishes from the table. 'Please excuse me. I will be right back. I must offer my prayers. We will continue this discussion when I return.'

Oh no we won't, Pochmann thought to himself, as he watched Rabeea's shapeless grey form exit the dining room, devoid of any desire to help her with the heavy tray she held in her bony hands.

Mohammed was practically on his knees as soon as she left the room. 'I'm so, so sorry, I am so sorry.'

'You see what I mean?' Mohammed Senior rose slowly to his feet. 'I will have a word with her.'

Pochmann waved his hand, shaking his head at the same time. 'It's not your fault. I can see she feels very passionately about her beliefs.' He himself firmly believed that religion was a private, somewhat embarrassing, matter. If you were foolish or sentimental enough to believe in God, you should at least have the good manners to keep it to yourself.

Mohammed lowered his head conspiratorially towards Pochmann. He whispered so that Mohammed Senior, who had not gone after Rabeea after all, couldn't hear. 'I don't know why she is like this. I cannot tell you how awkward it can be sometimes.'

'It's because she went to university,' boomed Mohammed Senior, ears sharp as a bat's.

'Oh?' said Pochmann. In and of itself, a university education should not be a problem, but he was curious to hear more.

'It's true.' Mohammed Senior's voice was choked with shame. 'She has a Masters in Sociology from Karachi University.'

Pochmann's eyebrows creased into furrows that would soon be permanently scarred into his skin. 'And?'

'You don't understand,' said Mohammed Senior. 'She has all sorts of *ideas*. She is not interested in taking care of the house, like a Pakistani woman should.'

Mohammed Junior said softly, 'She wants to go out and join the staff of a community clinic.'

'But what's wrong with . . .'

'Those places are terrible,' intoned Mohammed Senior. 'Those English women, they teach our women all the wrong things. How to wear jeans and T-shirts, and stop wearing the dupatta. They go out of the house at all hours of the day and night. And travel alone to other cities – alone! And ride in taxis!'

'But isn't that rather terrific? Wouldn't she be working to help people with their health?' Despite her antisocial behaviour, Pochmann was seized by a perverse desire to champion Rabeea's desires. 'Just like you?'

'She wants to teach people about *family planning*!' shouted Mohammed Senior.

'Family planning?'

'Yes. She thinks that all of us Pakistanis' problems come from cousin marriage. She says that the children are damaged! She doesn't listen to me when I tell her that children are a blessing from God!'

Mohammed Senior's face had gone purple with outrage. Mohammed Junior hung his head and looked as if he was ready to commit suicide. Pochmann's eyes flicked to the living room door; Rabeea could walk through at any minute. But Mohammed Senior's tongue had been loosened, and nothing could stop the stream of words that gushed out from the depths of his wounded soul.

'Family planning – can you believe it?' he fumed. 'Next thing, she will be telling women how to have abortions. Islam strictly forbids the killing of unborn children! When I got her married to my son, I thought, Now here is such a good, domesticated girl, from our own family. She will be hardworking and helpful. She will raise a good family of her own. But I was wrong. She does nothing but read books and go on the internet and read about politics!'

At that moment, Rabeea re-entered the drawing room. All three men shifted in their seats. Pochmann could see her eyes sharpen, her senses alert to the change in the room's atmosphere. One small drawing room filled with three foolish men would be, for most women, no challenge at all; for someone as thin-skinned and reactive as Rabeea, it would be like drinking a cup of tea in which someone had substituted vinegar for sugar.

But if she suspected anything, she didn't reveal it, thanks to the all-encompassing veil. And with that precise intuition, reading his resentment of her covered face, she zeroed in on Pochmann and said sweetly, 'Mr Pochmann, do you think Denmark was right to ban the burqa?'

All Pochmann's goodwill towards Rabeea evaporated like the early morning frost on the hood of his car as soon as the engine had heated up. 'I haven't exactly been following the news,' he said through clenched teeth.

'Oh, but it's in all the newspapers. I've been reading about it everywhere. They will fine and arrest any woman seen wearing it in public spaces. What do you think about that?'

Pochmann thought he could hear Mohammed Junior groaning very softly. He refused to look in his direction; he wouldn't be able to bear the shame written all over his young colleague's face. 'It doesn't sound unreasonable to me. It's their country, isn't it? Their laws.'

'But don't they believe in freedom of choice? If a woman chooses to wear a bikini, they don't mind that, but if she chooses to cover herself in public, they will send her to jail? I hate that double stranded. It is so unfair!' Her voice rose higher and higher, until it threatened to crack with hysteria. Mohammed Senior was clicking the beads of his rosary desperately as if counting out an infinite amount of money on an abacus, while Mohammed Junior sat with his elbows on the table, his head in his hands.

Pochmann saw the chance to drive in the knife, and went for it. 'Standard.'

'What?'

'Double *standard*. Not double stranded.'

She blinked three times in quick succession. Pochmann thought he could see a flicker of embarrassment in her eyes. Correcting her English was a supremely unfair move but, at that moment, all he could concentrate on was shutting her up, the only way he knew how.

'And it seems to me,' he added, 'that if they make women wear it in Saudi Arabia, it's only fair that they can ban it in Denmark, or France. Double *standard*, right?'

Rabeea breathed out very slowly, the burqa around her expanding and then deflating like the balloon pump in a ventilator. After a poison-filled moment, she said, 'Yes, Mr Pochmann. I know what a double standard is, thank you very much. Like in 9/11, when American people die, they are called *fallen heroes*. And when Muslims die in the War on Terror, they are called *collateral damage*. I believe *that* is what you call a double standard.'

Pochmann stared at her, and she stared back, undaunted and as regal and straight-backed as a queen.

'Now, if you will excuse me, it is time for the night prayer, Mr Pochmann. I wish you good evenings.'

She nodded at him, then swept out of the door. The sound of a dish shattering on the floor followed almost immediately after her exit.

Mohammed Senior raised his hands, prayer beads wound around the fingers of his right hand so tightly that they were turning blue. 'Do you see what I am up against? And this fool,' he shoved one shoulder back towards his son, 'won't say a word against her, even though she is full of disrespect for everyone. For me, for him and now, you can see, even for you. And when I ask him why, do you know what he says?'

Pochmann shook his head. He had no answer.

'*Because I love her*. That is his answer. *Love!*' He spat out the word like an errant pomegranate seed. 'This boy is more English than Pakistani, Mr Pochmann, no offence. But I hope you will understand. We call that being *angraiz*. For us, it is not a compliment.'

Mohammed Junior hadn't looked up once throughout the whole exchange, but a mulish look flashed in his eye that Pochmann caught just as his father pronounced the word *English*. And Pochmann, for the first time in the whole evening, could picture himself in the young man's shoes. Not because the scene made any sense to him. There were centuries, generations, *aeons* of distance between Pakistan and England – this evening had convinced him beyond any doubt of that. These were family dynamics he could never begin to comprehend.

But for the first time in many years, he remembered how he too had once been a young man, in love with a woman whom he had neither been able to understand nor control. The who, how, or the why didn't matter; only the feeling did.

'Yes,' he said, not in response to Mohammed Senior's plea, but in response to Mohammed Junior's eyes. 'I think I understand.'

Moments in Time

Sunah Ahmed

2 a.m.

The dull yellow glow from the streetlight shone through our cheap curtains, driving the sleep from my eyes. The door opened and I felt the mattress slump with Ali's weight as he got into bed. My gaze flitted to the digital clock on my bedside table: 2:05 a.m. flashed in red. I smelled shampoo, and a drop of water fell onto my cheek as he leaned over to adjust the sheets. I closed my eyes tightly and pretended to be asleep. I heard Ali sigh and move back to his side of the bed. A few minutes later he was snoring away. I turned to face him and stared hard at this familiar stranger.

*

9 a.m.

I was twenty-six today. As the kettle boiled, I thought back to my twentieth birthday, and meeting Isa for the very first time. Isa was everything I wasn't: cool, confident and charming. He had caught me off-guard outside the cinema when he asked me to grab a coffee with him. In an attempt to appear sophisticated, I ordered a cappuccino. He laughed when he saw my reaction as I slurped the drink, unable to conceal the fact that I hated the taste of coffee.

I remembered everything about our first date. How he had spoken so passionately about his studies, how difficult it was to be a writer in a materialistic society. I found myself getting lost in his eyes. I sat hypnotized by his voice and barely touched my chocolate muffin.

'Leena, have you made breakfast?'

Ali's gruff voice slammed me back into reality so hard I almost stumbled. I turned around to see the toast was burning.

'Just wait! I'll be a few minutes,' I called as I frantically started pouring the tea and scraping the burnt bits off of the toast.

I heard Ali's footsteps behind me. 'I smell burning, do you need some help?'

Irritation boiled up inside me. 'I don't need your help to make *toast,*' I said.

'Okay, I'll wait in the living room.' As Ali left the kitchen, I felt an unexpected sadness tinge my mood. He had forgotten. Of course, he had forgotten. Why had I ever thought he might remember that today was my birthday?

I balanced the cups of tea and toast on the tray and walked in on Ali engrossed in *Geo News*. I sighed inwardly. We had been repeating the same breakfast routine for three years, always eating together but providing one another with a minimal amount of attention. Ali crunched loudly on his buttered toast and slurped his tea in seconds. I tried not to shudder at the noise. I should have been used to it by now.

'Should we go out for dinner tonight?' I asked.

Ali's eyes never moved from the TV screen. 'What's wrong with eating here? We still have leftovers from last night.'

'That isn't the point,' I snapped. Trying to hold on to my patience, I added more calmly, 'I thought it might be nice, that's all.'

Ali still wasn't looking at me. 'We can go out if you like. I just think it's a waste.'

'Well, it's my . . . actually it doesn't matter. You're right, it would be a waste,' I said dully.

Sensing my disappointment, Ali turned to look at me. 'How about we go next Wednesday? Work is always quieter then. We can go to that new steak place that opened in town.'

I couldn't hide my frustration. 'I don't eat red meat.'

'Since when?'

'Since we got married, Ali!'

My husband looked as though he was going to say something, but then changed his mind. He got up and started to put his jacket on.

'Are you leaving already?' I asked.

He brushed the crumbs off his jeans before looking at me. 'I need to run a few errands before opening up. I will be home by eleven. Just leave my food in the oven.'

The door closed with a firm thud after him, leaving me alone to clean up the remains of breakfast.

10 a.m.

The minutes slowly ticked by as I tried to get the curry stain off Ali's shirt. It was useless. No matter how hard I scrubbed, the yellow smear refused to budge. In the end I gave up and flung it in the washing machine, knowing full well it would do nothing to remove the mark.

God, I hated the stench of Ali. The reek of mustard oil and sweat clung to his whole body. Sometimes he would be too tired to shower after work and I had to tell him to sleep in the spare room because I couldn't stand the smell. Even after he showered, I would catch fragments of his job. It was everywhere.

Isa was always immaculate. His hands were soft and betrayed a boy who hadn't had to work a day in his life. He always wore expensive cologne: a citrus smell, as if he had bathed in fresh oranges every night. If I closed my eyes I could see him standing in front of me, looking at me with eyes encased in thick black lashes, ones that girls would kill for. I could see him smiling. His hands reaching out to take . . .

The ding of the washing machine burst this image and brought me back to my mundane existence, standing in the kitchen. As predicted, the yellow stain was still there. If anything, it looked more obvious now against the bright white shirt. I flung it in the bin. I knew Ali would be upset when he found out, complaining that I had got rid of another 'good' shirt. He didn't care about imperfections; his work at the takeaway was dirty and stains were something he had become used to. I, on the other hand, had a hard time adapting.

11 a.m.

My parents were overjoyed when I got married. My mum had jubilantly declared to her friends that she was finally free. Passing me off to my husband meant she no longer needed to worry about my safety and chastity. As if I was incapable of safeguarding myself.

I knew it would be strange marrying a man I had only met on a handful of occasions but I told myself that arranged marriages had been happening for centuries. I was a product of one myself. In my naivety, I believed I would eventually fall in love with Ali.

No one had told me what marriage would really be like. Strangers congratulate you on your wedding — as if that is the hardest part: saying yes and signing the papers. Guests expect to see the bride cry at her wedding: 'An Asian bride should never smile,' the photographer had told me. So that's how a bride starts her married life, in tears. Once the glitz of the wedding disappears and everyday life begins, it regularly becomes a challenge to keep the tears away.

I remember going back to my parents' house a month after the wedding. I had walked into my old home and was hit by an overwhelming sense of nostalgia. It was home but it wasn't *my* home any more. I smelled dal, my favourite dish. My mum hugged me tightly and her scent was of rice and lavender. Her smell was so familiar, I burst out crying in her arms.

'Beta, what has happened?'

I had tried to keep quiet, but the words tumbled out. 'He isn't what I wanted. I can't do this.'

My mum's concerned voice had immediately switched to anger. 'What has he done, Leena? Has Ali hit you?'

'No, nothing like that. He is just always working and we have nothing in common.'

My mum had laughed with relief. 'That's why you're crying, Leena? Because he is trying to provide for you?'

'You don't understand. I thought we would spend time together and I would begin to develop feelings but he is never around long enough for us to even have a full conversation.'

My mum's arms had gripped my shoulders tightly. 'Leena, you need to get these romantic stories you have read in books out of your head. Women in our culture don't get love stories. Ali is a good man. He will be loyal and can look after you. You will grow to love him in time, the way I grew to love your dad.'

'Mum, what if I *don't* grow to love h—'

'Leena, that's enough!' She had hushed me before I could even finish. 'You need to stop this childish nonsense. What you want is not *real*. You are married to Ali and you need to make it work.'

I had shrugged her arms off my shoulders and wiped my tears with the sleeve of my shirt. That was the moment I understood that I was completely alone. No one wanted to know if I was unhappy. I had to live up to the illusion of the perfectly content Asian wife. I had followed my mum silently into the kitchen and we never spoke of the incident again.

*

1 p.m.

Ali wasn't a terrible person, as my mum reminded me on countless occasions. Her favourite line was that I was lucky to have found someone like him. Ali was solid and reliable (like a

Dyson vacuum cleaner). He had spent his whole life working hard and nothing had been handed to him on a plate. While that was all true and Ali had done very well with his work, he was utterly incompetent at keeping me happy. He was blissfully oblivious to my misery.

With Isa, it was always so easy. We would speak for hours on the phone, our topics ranging from literature to current affairs. He would text me every morning before university, telling me how beautiful I was, and leave me silly notes tucked into my favourite books. He urged me to pursue my dreams. I wanted to be an artist and I would take him to exhibitions every weekend. He once told me I was the finest work of art he had ever seen. It was a terrible line but it had made my insides melt.

Ali hadn't read a book in his life. 'Books won't pay the bills' — that's what he would say to me whenever I offered him one of my favourite titles. I struggled to remember the last time I had spoken to Ali about something other than dinner. Ali and I were not a match. I had trusted my parents to know best, and ended up with a man I knew I would never love. So instead I focused harder on my art, and spent my time daydreaming about the past. My life was a lie. I acted the dutiful wife and tried my best to respect my husband. I cooked and cleaned and to the outside world I guess we looked happy. Who cared if we actually *were* happy or not?

2 p.m.
The lonely cupcake sat on the kitchen table. I stuck a candle on top and lit a match. The candle burned brightly before settling into a sombre flame.

Isa's voice ran through my head. 'Make a wish, Leena.'

I shut my eyes tightly and blew out the candle. I wished to go back to my twenty-first birthday.

Isa and I had been walking in the park. The sun was shining and we decided to sit under the shade of some trees. He pulled a chain out of his pocket and wrapped it around my wrist. I had never been given a piece of jewellery before and the gesture took me by surprise. Isa reached for my hand and squeezed it tightly.

'Leena, I love you.'

He said it in such a matter-of-fact way that it took a few moments to register what he had said to me. I had imagined him saying these words, but I was shocked when he did.

'I love you too,' I whispered into the empty room.

The smell of smoke filled the air. I pulled out the candle and bit into the cake. I always did like to eat my feelings.

3 p.m.

Art never failed to relax me. I love the way a single painting can tell many different stories. Van Gogh had always been my favourite. He was a disturbed man but even in the darkest times his work was breathtaking. His pain brought so much pleasure. And it was his pain that helped make him famous. Happy people never make good artists. It's a job for the damaged.

I had taken over the garage and made it into my art studio. I gave sketching classes to children at weekends. I enjoyed teaching – it was one of the few things I was good at. Having my own child was something I had pushed to the back of my mind, but teaching helped me realize I could make a difference.

Art was just another thing that demonstrated the chasm separating Ali from me. While Isa was able to understand the beauty of paintings, Ali struggled to suppress his yawns whenever we walked past a gallery.

Ali called art a hobby, a hobby he saw no point in pursuing.

I remembered showing him some work by the Impressionists and asking what he thought.

He had barely glanced at the first painting before saying, 'The picture is blurred – how is that art? I could paint better than that.'

'That's the whole point: it is meant to be an *impression*, not an exact depiction.'

'Maybe they just couldn't paint and pretended they did it on purpose.'

It had taken every fibre in my body not to scream at Ali for his lack of respect. I had to remind myself that it wasn't his fault; he just couldn't fathom anything unrelated to work or food.

*

5 p.m.

I spooned the pasta onto my plate and waited for it to cool. Isa loved Italian cuisine. Every Friday after we had both finished our lectures at university, we would sit in the library and I would pull out the tub of pasta I had cooked the night before. We would sit huddled together between the stacks of dusty books, sharing the food, completely content in each other's company. I had prayed nothing would change.

Isa and I had a plan: graduate, get married, move out of Glasgow and find jobs. It was a plan I had intended to stick to; in fact, my whole life revolved around this plan. But people change and plans have to change along with them.

6 p.m.

I stared at my graduation photo hanging up in the living room. I barely recognized myself in it; my hair was cropped and I was beaming. My parents were standing on either side, looking equally proud.

Isa and I had gone out for a meal that evening. I made an excuse to my parents about needing to see a friend and had skipped the family dinner. They were disappointed but I had promised we would go out together a few days later. I just wanted to share the special moment with Isa. That night, I was filled with happiness, but it was tinted with melancholy because I knew he and I now wouldn't be able to spend every day at university together. Isa had seemed quiet and lacked his usual chatty manner, but I assumed he was thinking about the same thing.

I had stared at his untouched food in confusion. It wasn't like Isa to leave a dish uneaten, especially when I had purposely chosen his favourite restaurant.

'Don't you like your food?'

I seemed to have brought him out of his daze because he stopped playing with his linguine and put his fork down.

'Leena, I have some news. I don't know how to tell you this. It may not be what you're expecting but I got accepted into a two-year advanced writing programme.'

I almost choked on my mouthful. 'Isa! That's amazing news. I didn't realize you were even applying for further studies.'

Isa looked like he was about to throw up. My heart skipped a beat.

'What's wrong?' I asked.

'It's in New York.'

I put my fork down. 'As in America?'

Isa leaned in and tried to take my hand but I brushed it off.

'It means I can work with the best writers in the world.'

'It's for two years, Isa.'

'I know this isn't what we were planning, but I can't turn it down. It could help build my career.'

I can still remember the excitement in his eyes; he wanted this so badly. I knew then that I wouldn't be able to stop him.

'Maybe I could look for jobs there? And we can wait a little longer until we settle down,' I started.

Isa dropped his gaze, avoiding looking at me, and I felt my stomach drop.

'Leena, I love you, but I think this is something I have to do alone.'

I was taken aback by his response but I tried not to let it upset me.

'I guess we can still call and message. Two years isn't that long when you think about it, and you will come back to visit.'

Isa looked miserable. 'Leena, when I mean alone, I mean *completely* alone.'

'I don't understand. Just tell me clearly what you want to do.' I tried to remain calm but even I could hear the quiver in my voice.

Isa was silent and I felt tears sting my eyes.

'You want to break up, don't you?' My voice was barely a whisper but I knew Isa heard every word.

'Leena, you are the best thing that has happened to me, but aren't you worried that your life is already mapped out for you? We are so young and we have already planned our futures. What if that isn't the way life is supposed to be? I don't want to have any regrets.'

My heart broke at his words.

'You think I'm a regret?'

'No, I just — I know this is something I have to do.'

'And what am I supposed to do, wait for you?' I hoped he would say yes; a yes would mean we could still be together. A yes was all I wanted.

Instead: 'No, I could never ask that of you. I want you to be happy and if you meet someone else then I only wish you the best.'

7 p.m.

Memories are strange, they can comfort you or haunt you.

I cried for months after Isa left. In the beginning he messaged frequently, telling me how much he missed me and how sorry he was for hurting me. I would spend hours on his social media, stalking any girl who commented on his picture. Eventually, heartbreak turned to bitter disdain. I deleted him, all remnants of him, from my world. I couldn't handle seeing how great his life was without me. I cut ties, secretly hoping he would reach out and make contact, but he never did. I thought he would change his mind, that he would realize how much he loved me and not want to be apart, but it didn't happen. I waited six months before realizing Isa was never going to regret his decision. Isa had decided I wasn't enough and, in my rejection, I decided the best thing to do was find someone else.

Ali offered me something Isa couldn't — commitment. Isa was partying, writing, and most likely sleeping with anything that had a pulse. He was over me. I had to move on, and I did.

9 p.m.

I put Ali's dinner in the oven and hoped the roast chicken wouldn't burn. I was a terrible cook but Ali never complained. He would happily munch away at anything I put in front of him. Ali was security, and I knew he would never even think of hurting me. I wished that was enough for me.

Life hadn't turned out how I had envisioned it, but then again — who really did have the perfect life? I knew Isa hadn't married; he was far too busy for that. I suppose I took some comfort from the fact that he hadn't settled down with another woman; it proved to me that no one was ever enough for him.

11:45 p.m.

Ali sat on the edge of the bed.

'Leena? Are you awake?'

I was, but I pretended I had been sleeping solidly for hours. 'I am now. I left dinner in the oven.'

'Yeah, I ate it, but I want to talk.' He switched the bedside lamp on.

I opened my eyes and yawned dramatically. 'Was there something wrong with the chicken I cooked?'

'It isn't about dinner,' He handed me a clumsily wrapped brown package. 'Happy birthday, Leena.'

I propped myself up against the headboard. 'I thought you'd forgotten.'

'I would never forget your birthday. I set a reminder on my phone.'

His reply had me stumped; I couldn't believe he had remembered. A smile spread across my face as I hurriedly unwrapped the package. A book settled in my hands. I read the author's name and stared hard at the cover.

'I know you like his books. He was doing a signing this afternoon and I told him how big a fan my wife is,' Ali explained with a proud grin.

I didn't speak. I couldn't.

'He is a nice guy, a little short. He told me he would be here all week doing workshops, and to tell you to come in and chat to him. He's keen to meet his fans.'

Forcing myself to speak, I asked, 'Ali, did you mention my name?'

'Well, yeah. He asked for it when signing the book. That's why I was away early – I didn't want to miss his event.'

I opened the book, and there it was. There was no denying it now. I would have recognized his writing anywhere, even if he hadn't written the message:

To Leena, thinking of you, Isa Mazhar x

'Is something wrong? He is the right author?' Ali asked, looking confused at my reaction.

I swallowed the bubble of emotion that had risen at the back of my throat and nodded. 'Yeah, it is the right person. I never knew he was in Glasgow.' Putting the book aside, I reached over and switched the lamp off, before Ali grew suspicious of the tears that were forming in my eyes. He got into bed beside me.

'Did I do something wrong? Do you want me to take a shower?' He sounded so anxious.

'No Ali, it's okay. I am just really tired tonight.'

I turned my back to him and closed my eyes tightly as the tears streamed down my face.

2 a.m.

Thinking of you – what did that mean? Maybe it was something he wrote on all his signed books – a little bit of intimacy between reader and writer. But what if . . . what if he really meant it? What if throughout the five years we had been apart, Isa had also been thinking of me? Wondering what I was doing and hoping to find me again. My stomach lurched at the thought and my heart started to race. I stepped out of bed and walked towards the door, careful not to wake Ali who as usual was blissfully unaware of my thoughts.

I mean, how could Isa even have got in touch with me? I wasn't on social media and I had cut contact with all mutual friends not long after he moved to America. Meeting up with people he was still speaking to and being told about his successes was something I couldn't handle. It wasn't as if I was unaware of what he was up to. I bought every book he published and watched his online interviews, but that was all in private, away from prying eyes. I had never expected our paths to collide and he hadn't been back to Glasgow in years. Now here was Ali reconnecting us; the irony made me laugh.

I wonder what Isa would have thought of Ali? At six foot four, Ali would have loomed over Isa. God, he had been wearing that hideous jacket today, but at least he had a clean shirt on. I could imagine Isa looking him up and down; presentation was everything to him. Isa was all about his suits and designer labels, and with the success of his books he could afford them. But Ali was handsome in the conventional sense of the word.

He had straight white teeth and black hair that curled slightly after he showered. Why did I even care what Isa thought of Ali? What did it matter?

I pulled out my laptop and switched it on. The familiar gentle purr sounded as the home screen appeared. My fingers seemed to be working without me as I punched the name Isa Mazhar into Google: 489,000 results found. Luckily for me there was only one Isa Mazhar, author. It wasn't long before I found his homepage detailing his recent visit to Taylor's Bookshop. He was far too bourgeois to have done a signing at Waterstones. My eyes lingered on the sentence Upcoming dates for workshops available here, book now. I clicked in and booked for the 3 p.m. slot the following day. I filled in the information boxes:

First Name: Leena
Second Name: Din
Email Address: Leena789@hotmail.com

I then deleted Din and replaced it with Baig, my maiden name. My arrow hovered above Confirm booking.

'Leena, where are you?'

I heard Ali call my name and slammed the laptop shut.

'I went to get a drink of water,' I shouted back cheerfully. 'Is everything okay?' I walked back into the room, glad for the darkness which hid my burning cheeks.

'Yeah. It's just I woke up suddenly and when you weren't next to me, I got worried. Are you feeling okay?'

I nodded, even though Ali would not be able to see in the darkness. 'Of course, everything's fine. I just felt thirsty.'

Ali didn't seem convinced. Why was it on this occasion he wanted to ask a lot of questions?

'Leena, I know you think I don't notice anything but I can tell something is wrong. You know you can talk to me. I'm your husband.'

I felt my chest tighten up as I opened my mouth to answer. 'I know, Ali. You are my husband and always will be. Nothing will change that.'

In the darkness the streetlight hit his mouth and I saw a smile creep to his lips. 'I can't remember the last time you called me your husband.' I heard him chuckle to himself before saying, 'Wife, come back to bed.'

My heart ached. 'Just give me a second, I think I left the tap running.' And I sprinted out before he could say another word.

I walked back to my laptop and lifted the screen. Error, your session has timed out. Please rebook. I closed the webpage and switched off the laptop before heading back to bed with my husband, Ali.

Frida's Breakfast

Roopa Farooki

Frida has terrible dreams. She is so full of terrible dreams that she thinks she might burst open with them. Her boyfriend (she can't say fiancé, it feels too final, it's a word which seems to have a noose attached to it) thinks that her shifting at night, her troubled sleep, her laboured breath are because of the baby. In fact, they are all because of her dreams — although she usually dreams about the baby, and so in a way he is right. She hates the way that Salim always seems to be right. She hates the way he asserts this with cheerful, easy confidence. 'And you know I'm right,' he'll say, tossing the sentence off over his shoulder, not even bothering to see if it has landed. She hates this almost as much as she hates her dreams.

Frida dreams that she has left the baby in a forest and walked away, picking strawberries nonchalantly while wearing a blood-red cape. She dreams that she wakes, starving, and sees a bowl of dried wafers by her bedside, each with the pale purity of Communion host. Somehow, she knows that these wafers were once the baby, but she is too hungry to resuscitate the baby from dried wafers to flesh and blood. Wolf-like, she eats them instead, gorging herself with savage irreverence.

Or she dreams that she is bulimic, as she was before the pregnancy established itself and her vomiting became involuntary in her first trimester. Instead of throwing up her habitual mess of biscuits and chip butties, she is throwing up the baby. She is purged once more, and with the acid burn in her mouth feels the dark delight that this always gave her. Clean inside and out. Cured of her insidious pregnancy.

When her friends ask after the pregnancy, ask how she's doing, she laughs at their concern and says with teenage insouciance, 'What's the big deal? It's not as though I'm *sick*.' But she is. Sick, sick, sick. Infected with terrible dreams.

Frida gets up later than the other students who share her staircase. The term is almost finished, and she isn't bothering to attend morning lectures any more. She handed in her last paper a few days ago and now has nothing to take care of, apart from her final wedding preparations, and trying to eat enough calories to fatten the baby. She carefully cleans the communal shower before she uses it, scrubbing it over a dozen times until she is satisfied, and then she washes herself thoroughly. After that, she cleans the shower all over again, disregarding an impatient banging on the door. Frida has always been meticulously tidy, and now suspects that she is becoming compulsively so. It gives her a sense of control, something she no longer has over her body. Housework as therapy, she thinks bitterly. Christ, she's already turned into a housewife; worse, she's turning into her mother. If she had just an ounce of proper teenage rebellion in her she'd have started shoplifting instead.

Frida wraps a towel around her (it barely fits, and her breasts are now so heavy and low that she can't tuck it neatly in at her cleavage like she used to do but is forced to clutch it together with one hand) before padding back to her room in her slippers. She dresses in her college tracksuit bottoms, which are too hot for the weather but the only casual trousers that seem to fit, and a patterned kameez in faded violet that her mother had carelessly torn and thrown out, but which Frida had rescued and repaired.

She makes herself breakfast, just some buttered toast with a mug of milky decaf. She resents that she is no longer allowed scrambled eggs on the toast, or proper coffee. Her mother thinks that these rules are stupid, but her mother is no one to judge her, because her mother is stupid too, and blundered through her own youthful pregnancy without even knowing what the rules were, or even that there were rules in the first place. Unlike her mother, Frida is doing this by the book. And so she is excluding scrambled eggs and caffeine and wine and sushi and unpasteurized cheeses, and forcing herself to choke down milk and wheatgerm and iron supplements. She even eats a weekly can of sardines, like medicine, munching on the revolting little bones for extra calcium. She is studying baby manuals and catalogues in as much detail as her coursework. She is making an event of her mistake, celebrating it with baby showers and a big, garish wedding, so that it looks like she intended it all along, so that people won't pity her for being just another knocked-up teenager, so that she won't pity herself either. She's announcing to everyone that it is her goddamn dream come true. She is trying not to care that probably nobody is buying this, not even her more naive college friends, not even her mother.

If only I could be a different sort of freak, thinks Frida. Like that grey-haired hippie woman in town who chants tunelessly on the street corners, wears a woven blanket and claims to speak to ghosts. Why couldn't she be a publicly spiritual nut, instead of a private psychotic?

The worst dream she has is when she wakes in her college room to see that Salim and the baby are dead, and she has no idea whether or not she did it; she has no idea whether or not it is real. Apart from the dead bodies, her room is recreated in alarmingly precise detail: her oversized comb with the two bent prongs, her Punjabi jewellery box with the cracked lid that she has disguised with green silk fabric and small embroidered mirrors, the black ceramic bowl which she has lovingly glued back together, and her moth-eaten, once-pink-now-grey bunny with the rattling chest, a line of childish stitches holding in the stuffing.

It takes her a moment, on waking, to lose the chilling authenticity of the grisly scene, and to remind herself that the baby is not yet born, so it could only be a dream. She doesn't want to think about when the baby arrives, when the lines between her dreams and reality become less easy to draw. She doesn't want to think about whether she will continue to kill her baby and her lover in her head at night, and what she will feel when she wakes to see them, sleeping soundly, one in a crib and the other by her side. She doesn't want to consider whether her first thought on waking, on crossing the blurry border between dreams and reality, will be relief or disappointment. There are lines that should not be drawn, so they cannot be crossed.

Frida's boyfriend slept in his own room last night, as her fidgeting bothered him, but he knocks on her door now, unnecessarily saying, 'Knock, knock,' cheerfully. It amazes her that less than a year ago she found the 'Knock, knock' charming; now it makes her grit her teeth. In fact, it makes her want to knock, knock his teeth out with a cricket bat. Salim is a keen cricketer, and keeps a bat in his room; a bit heavy for her to handle, she thinks, but it would do the job.

She smiles, the inappropriate, secretive smile of a sadistic child ripping the wings off bugs, and this smile is what Salim sees as he walks into her unlocked room. He smiles back and she feels suddenly ashamed; reminds herself that it isn't real – none of the evil stuff in her head is real. What is real is this, that she is a heavily pregnant girl eating toast in her room, the day before her wedding. That she is smiling at her boyfriend, and he is smiling back at her. She feels a burst of affection towards Salim for accepting her for what she appears to be, without excavating deeper under her skin and unearthing the bodies she has buried every morning when she wakes. This acceptance, she thinks, this simple trust, must be a type of love.

'Oh, hey there,' she says.

'All right, mate?' he says. He calls everyone 'mate' regardless of gender and intimacy; she supposes he likes the democracy of it, and it saves him having to remember names. He is wearing his college tracksuit bottoms too, and the grey T-shirt hanging off his slender frame is printed with an image of Malcolm X holding a gun: it bears the legend **BY ANY MEANS NECESSARY**. He must have been running, for he has the earthy, acrid scent of sweat, and he is still bouncing on his heels, as though he hasn't quite finished. His hair is damp, and she wonders whether he wet it in the sink on his way up to her room; she has a sudden, itching desire to go back to the communal bathroom to clean it again.

'Did you want to come out for breakfast?' he says. 'Big day tomorrow. Most important meal, blah, blah, blah.'

'I've already had breakfast. Obviously. Duh,' she replies, like a stupid teenager. I *am* a stupid teenager, she remembers. She should be allowed to pour scornful derision on reasonable requests, and finish every sentence with 'Duh', 'Meh' or, like Salim, 'Blah, blah, blah'. She should be allowed to fill ordinary words like 'Score' and 'Fuck' with rainbows of meaning. She should be allowed to say 'Yeah, no' or '*That's* what I'm talking about' without sounding ironic. She should be allowed to stay up all night, kiss random guys she meets at clubs, enjoy stinking kebabs with chilli sauce and pass out on the grass until morning.

Her eyes become damp with regret, that impending marriage and motherhood have already withdrawn all these strange gifts from her. Her parents never even had these gifts in the first place; they were distant cousins cajoled and jostled into a respectable arranged marriage before they had even finished their degrees, but she has now been trapped just as surely as they were. The bitter irony is that her own trap wasn't set by comically severe aunties or stifling tradition, but by the very freedoms denied to her parents: the freedom to move away from home to study, the freedom to have irresponsible sex with an otherwise painfully responsible boy from the next staircase along. Just because she thought he was cute, and he thought that she was pretty.

'It's not breakfast if it's not fried,' says Salim, looking pityingly at her toast. 'You could just come along with me anyway. I could use the company, and I'm not going to see you the rest of the day, with all this last-minute crap you've got us doing.'

Frida looks at him with surprise. 'You're going to be stuck with me every day for the rest of your life. Are you really bothered if I have breakfast with you today?'

'You're joking, right?' says Salim. 'Of course I'm bothered.' He walks over to her and pats her on the belly. 'So how's my girl?' he asks. 'Are you okay?'

For a moment Frida assumes he must be talking to the baby, and only responds when he looks at her questioningly. 'Yeah, no. I don't know. I feel kind of rubbish. I didn't sleep again.'

'Aw, mate,' says Salim sympathetically. 'Anything I can do?'

He puts his arms around her, under the kameez, and when his hand brushes the bare skin at her waist she shrinks away, drawing in her flesh as much as the three-kilo weight in her belly will allow. It isn't the attempt at comfort that bothers her, it's the contact. Something about being touched in this last trimester just seems to disgust her.

'You could bugger off and get started on your to-do list, so I don't have to worry about it,' she says, shrugging him off. 'I've still got the favours to wrap.'

'No problem,' says Salim. 'I'll sort my stuff out after breakfast.' He rubs her back affectionately. 'When are you heading over to the hotel?'

'Just after lunch,' Frida replies. 'I know it's early, but I want to . . .'

'Yeah, I know,' nods Salim. 'I can't wait either. It's going to be one hell of a party tomorrow. Best day of our lives.'

Frida smiles weakly. In fact, she had been going to say, 'I just want to get there and get it over with,' but he doesn't need to know that. He is too good at this, she thinks, too good. It must be a show, just like the one she is putting on. He must lower his shoulders with a sigh of relief once he is alone, just as she does, taking a break from this tired little play. Day after day, performance after performance, acting the role of the loving, supportive fiancé – that word with the noose – and finally the husband – that word which closes the hard, tight knot over her throat, that word which drops open the trapdoor and leaves her broken and swinging like a painted puppet on a string.

'And you know I'm right,' he adds, ruffling and then smoothing out her hair before he leaves, as if she were an exasperating kid sister rather than kissing her like a lover. Once they started dating, this habit of his used to annoy her. But now she is grateful for it, for the lack of intimacy, as she doesn't need to pretend or to respond.

She goes to the sink in the corner of the room and washes the skin that he touched on her stomach, again, and again, and again. From being typically prickly but unalarmed by his arrival, with his departure it feels as if each groaning cell in her body is both panicked and stricken with dreadful lethargy. She is already sitting down, but everything deep inside just wants to sit down too, to collapse into a tangled wet heap, her baby, her blood, her bones.

She calms herself by counting all the things she can see in her room; however, she is still not calm when she has finished, and so she counts to a thousand. It is what she does in the night, to pass the wakeful moments between her dreams. This takes her fifteen minutes or so to do, and every milestone of one hundred satisfies her, and the downward slope after five hundred fills her with achievement and impatience. She counts quicker than she breathes, and remembers odd things, a dead squirrel in the park when she was six years old, her embarrassment at a sports day in junior school when her casually-dressed mother was mistaken for her sibling, the Barbie cake with a gown made of pink-iced layers of vanilla sponge and buttercream, the boy she kissed at a party when she was thirteen, just to see what it would be like, the smell of dusty, sleeping books in the reference section of the school library, the metallic taste of cider and black in the college bar.

Her mobile rings while she is counting, and she sees that it is her mother calling. Her silly, undignified mother, who infuriates Frida with the casual way she blunders through life. Her mother, who wasted her own education, choosing to remain a homemaker, and whose most serious concerns these days seem to revolve around shopping and the soaps on TV. Frida feels a wash of dread, already bored to tears at the prospect of having to endure another senseless conversation with her. She lets out a sigh of relief when the phone stops ringing, and resumes her counting. She vaguely wonders how many more times she will need to count to one thousand before this day and night are over, before she is Salim's wife, before that noose tightens and that trapdoor falls open. The numbers ripple by, as though she is trailing her hand in cool water. She is almost done.

Frida begins to wrap favours for the wedding, a dull job she actually enjoys; she finds the repetition soothing. She has a bundle of unfeasibly bright sari off-cuts, swirling and shimmering with bold prints and embroidery, that she picked up at the market in Tooting the last time she was in London. She cuts the raggedly hemmed pieces into neat, shining circles, placing the gold and silver sugared almonds in the centre of each, twisting the material into pretty pouches. She ties each of them with a silk ribbon and bow. A few dozen favours are already set out in a box, so she just has another hundred to do.

Her phone rings again, and this time Frida doesn't ignore it. She knows that it will ring all morning otherwise. She picks it up, her face already hardening, her mouth thinning with intolerance. 'Hi, Amma, what is it?'

'Hello, sweetie! I'm so glad I got hold of you, I was getting worried. Didn't you get the message I left about . . .'

'Yeah, Amma, I did. I sent you a text saying that everything's fine, you don't need to do anything.'

'Oh sorry, sweetie, I didn't see the text,' says her mother.

'No worries. Is there anything else, Amma? I'm a bit busy with wedding stuff,' says Frida pointedly.

'Sweetie, can I ask you something about that? It's just that, you know we love you and . . . look, don't feel you *have* to, if you see what I mean.'

Frida sucks in her breath impatiently. 'Amma, you're blabbering. So I don't understand what you mean. I haven't a clue.'

'Well, it's just that . . . you know,' her mother starts to repeat, and Frida doesn't even bother to hide her irritation.

'Just spit it out, Amma, for God's sake!' she snaps, adding, 'I haven't got all day. I haven't got the *time* for this.'

'That's enough, young lady,' says her mother after a brief and injured silence, struggling to pull herself together. The indignation lasts no longer than her next deep breath, however, and when she speaks again, she sounds loving and cautious once more. 'Sweetie, Frida-moni, I just need to know something.'

She is so cautious that Frida suddenly wonders whether her mother dreads calling her just as much as she dreads her mother's calls. That she is stuck with Frida, in the same way Frida feels stuck with her. It suddenly unsettles the girl, who has never before doubted the sincerity and unwavering nature of her mother's love, despite her foolishness, her magazine-and-shopping frivolity. Frida has always assumed that all this annoying love was something she would have to endure, that it would always be buzzing insistently around her, however many times she swatted it away. So: how would she feel if the buzzing were no longer there? Relieved, for a moment. And then she would be unnerved by the silence, a silence which would be broken by nothing apart from her boyfriend's cheery 'Knock, knock,' and a baby's fearful wailing.

'What is it, Mama?' Frida asks, calling her Mama as she did when she was little, placing it before her feet as a peace-offering. An apology. We can never be truly cruel to our mothers and get away with it, she thinks. We can outgrow almost everything but that particular guilt.

'I just need to know – you are doing this for the right reasons, aren't you, sweetie? Because you want to, not because you feel you have to? I mean, I know it worked out with your daddy and me, getting married so early. But back then, it didn't feel like we had that much choice. But you do. There's no disgrace to it. No – I hate using this word – but no *dishonour*. You can choose not to.'

'Am-ma!' cries Frida, stopping her in adolescent outrage, as though her mother has just embarrassed her in public. 'You are *so* not doing this to me! You are not messing with my head the day before my wedding. The reception's booked, Amma! Don't you know how much Daddy's paid for all this? We've invited a hundred and fifty people. We've got a caterer. We've got an ice sculpture, for God's sake!'

'I know all that, sweetie,' her mother perseveres, 'but it's not about that. It's not about the money, or the guests or the ice sculpture. It's about you and Salim, and the rest of your lives.'

'No, no, no!' says Frida, shaking her head violently. 'We're not doing this, Mother. Look, I've got to go.' She doesn't care that she said Mother. She doesn't care that she said it as coldly as one might say Bitch. Simply because her supposedly silly mother has surprised her with her perception, and humbled her with the truth. Guilt, and more guilt.

'Frida-moni, don't hang up,' her mother says apologetically. 'I didn't mean to upset you, sweetie, you know that.'

'I've got to go, I'm late for the wedding planner,' Frida lies, not quite kindly enough. She waits a moment, says, 'Bye then,' and puts down her phone. She looks at the evidence of industry around her, the sweets in the jar, the circles of fabric, the silk ribbon. How pathetic it all seems, her wedding reduced to a handful of gold and silver sweets in a pretty piece of cloth. How pathetic, to have had the whole charade laid bare, by a blundering, well-meaning call from her mother.

The baby, possibly woken by the conversation, by her mother's agitation, begins to move agitatedly itself. Frida can feel a pummelling under her ribs, a foot or a knee. 'Stop it,' she says to the baby. 'Stop it!' she practically shouts. 'That's enough! That's enough, young lady.' She knows that her mother is right: she isn't ready for this, for a party, for a baby, for the flat that she and Salim will be moving into together.

She looks at the sweets twinkling with sudden, brittle menace behind the glass of the jar, and feels the urge to eat them all, every last one, and then to throw them up into a mashed-up metallic mess in the sink, and then clean, scrub and scrape every trace of them away. She digs her nails into her palms, quietening herself with the pain, then takes a deep breath and begins to count again.

Her phone rings once more, and she sees that it is just Salim calling. She answers cautiously. 'Hey there,' she says.

'Hey, mate, I've got the place cards here. Did you want me to write them up too?'

'Are you kidding – with your handwriting? No one will know where they're meant to be sitting.'

'Okay, if you're sure,' says Salim. He sounds relieved.

'I'm sure,' says Frida. 'I'll do them later.'

She is sure, after all, she decides; she has to be. She looks around her room, filled with damaged and torn things that she has saved and tried to mend: the comb, the jewellery box, the ceramic pot, the rattling pink-grey bunny, even the cheaply pretty violet shirt she is wearing. She has always been good at fixing damaged things, and this time, she will have to fix herself. She won't have one sweet or five hundred. She won't yell at the baby. She won't take her mother's advice. She will do whatever useless tasks she has assigned herself to do today, the day before her wedding, and with the repetition, with the practice, she will eventually do them well.

In the way that we do everything well with practice, until it becomes as unremarkable as breathing.

As unremarkable as counting to a thousand.

As unremarkable as killing your baby and your lover in your head.

A Simple Nature

Inayah Jamil

'Mariam! Hurry up, they will be here soon,' Mum called.

'Coming!' Mariam replied, rushing down the stairs. 'Mm, the food smells great.'

Mum didn't say anything, but Mariam could see she was fighting panic even as she smiled back at her.

'What's wrong?' Mariam asked.

'Nothing, beta, just help me get this place organized and tidied before our guests arrive for Hanna's rishta.'

Of course, her rishta, Mariam thought grumpily. How could I forget?

'Mum, I feel like you guys don't want me to get married,' she said aloud.

'What makes you think that, beta?'

'Well, you're so focused on Hanna that you've forgotten all about me.' Mariam's voice cracked almost imperceptibly.

'Beta, I have told you many times that after we get Hanna married, we will do the same for you. Anyway, there's no rush.

You've got plenty of time after you finish your studies,' Mum reassured her.

'Come on, by then I'll be coming up to twenty-three! How am I going to find someone if you and Dad are solely focused on getting Hanna a rishta?'

'Beta, don't worry. You have many cousins back home. You can marry one of them,' Mum replied distractedly.

Mariam pointed out that she had no interest in marrying a relative from Pakistan. Her mother brushed off her objections, saying she didn't have time for this as the guests would soon be arriving. Complete silence followed. Mariam didn't say a word as her mother busied herself arranging the food trays in order to avoid further conversation. With a sigh of resignation, Mariam moved forward to help her.

'Beta, please try and get along with Hanna – even if she won't make the effort.'

Mariam sighed and said she would try her best. She looked around the kitchen, asking after her younger sister Amara's whereabouts.

'She's playing in the back garden,' Mum replied. 'Tell her to come inside now.'

'Will do.' Mariam went to the back door, stepped outside and saw the girl riding her bike up and down. 'Amara! You need to come inside now.'

Amara used her most petulant voice to ask why.

'Because our guests will be here very soon and if you don't come in now, there won't be any food left for you,' Mariam warned her.

'Fine.' Amara dragged her bike into the garage and stomped inside. She and Mariam went through from the kitchen to the living room.

'Oh great! It's *you* again,' pronounced an annoyed voice the moment Mariam stepped into the room.

Mariam found Hanna standing before her, looking her stepsister up and down in disgusted amazement. 'You're not wearing *that* to my rishta, are you?'

'Yes, I am. Why, what's wrong with it?'

Hanna stared at Mariam with wide eyes. 'It's very simple-looking.'

Mariam fired back that 'simple' was the look she was going for. She had promised her mum she wouldn't fight with Hanna, but her stepsister never made it easy.

'Don't you have anything fancy to wear?' Hanna bit out. 'It looks like you haven't made any effort at all. You're not even wearing makeup.' She put her hands on her hips and shook her head in her usual condescending way. 'Honestly, Mariam, no guy is going to want to marry you with a face like *that*. You need to be in it to win it, if you want to live a happy life.'

Mariam rolled her eyes. 'I'm pretty sure that's not true, and anyway, true beauty comes from within.' She smirked. 'Plus, I only wear that stuff when the occasion is really *special*.'

It didn't take long for Hanna's face to darken with anger. 'Oh, so you don't think this occasion is special enough to look a little put-together?'

'You know that's not what I meant so calm it,' Mariam shot back. 'And for your information, I'm wearing mascara and lip gloss: I *have* made an effort.'

Hanna looked ready to commit murder. 'Effort!' she shrieked. 'You call that effort? You could have tried a bit harder.'

By now, Mariam had had enough of Hanna's tantrum. 'At least I embrace what I naturally have, not like you: caking it on till your face is barely visible.'

Amara was listening in to their conversation. Being young, she found the fight funny rather than alarming.

'Excuse me,' Hanna sneered. 'You wish you had this face.'

'Actually, no, I don't. And you know what? I never will.'

Before Hanna could retort, the bell rang. Hearing it, she let out an excited yelp and ran to the door, flicking her hair behind her and smoothing down her excessively embroidered kurta.

'Oh, great! They're here,' Mariam murmured snidely.

Amara looked confused at her sarcasm, so Mariam distracted the little girl by pinching her cheek.

*

'Mariam? *Mariam!* Who are you looking at?' Sunni whispered as she clicked her fingers in front of her friend's face.

'What? Nobody.'

'Then pay attention to the lecturer. You haven't written down a single word since you came in.'

'I'm sorry, what are we meant to be doing again?'

'Well, maybe if you'd been concentrating and hadn't been staring at that guy the whole time, you would know,' Sunni teased her.

'I wasn't staring. I was observing,' Mariam argued.

'Sure. Like I'm supposed to believe that,' Sunni scoffed, tossing her head.

'Who is he?' Mariam asked, looking once more at the tall, dark-haired boy sitting across the lecture hall. 'I've never seen him attend any of our classes before.'

'He's probably new.'

The lecturer then announced that the class was coming to an end and gave them their work for the coming week. Students started packing their bags and standing up as a soft chatter broke out across the hall.

'Shall we go for lunch, then?' Sunni asked, swinging her bag over her shoulder.

Mariam watched the new boy walk out of the lecture hall.

'Yeah, let's do it,' she replied.

*

'If you could all take your seats, please, we will begin today's session,' the lecturer announced over the noise of students struggling in.

Mariam and Sunni hurried to the back of the hall.

'You revised for your other classes?' Sunni quizzed her.

'Yup, it's all up here.' Mariam tapped her head.

Sunni chuckled.

Something caught Mariam's eye. 'Hey, look. It's that guy again. He's in our afternoon class too.'

Sunni wasn't half as interested as Mariam. 'Maybe he follows the same timetable,' she drawled, playing with her pencil.

'Maybe,' Mariam said pensively, still gazing at the mysterious boy.

'For your next assignment, you will write creative pieces that will be presented to the group and then collected in a portfolio,' the lecturer revealed. 'This assignment will be done in pairs. I want to see you come up with an original topic and work together as a team.'

'You and me.' Mariam grinned at Sunni.

'Sure.' Sunni beamed back.

'On the noticeboard I have written your names and who you will be working with,' the lecturer said.

'What!' Mariam exclaimed, her smile fading. 'No! Why would she do this to us?'

'I know.' Sunni was put out. 'We would have nailed this assignment together.'

'Come on, let's see who we've been put with.'

As the friends made their way to the crowded noticeboard, the good-looking boy who had caught Mariam's eye approached them, looking hesitant.

'Hey, you're Mariam, right?' he asked her directly.

Mariam had to take a moment to reply, she was so surprised that he knew who she was. 'Yes, that's me.'

The boy smiled. 'It says on the board we're working together.'

Mariam fought to keep her cool. 'Oh? Okay. Nice one.' She could sense Sunni simpering beside her. She tried to keep her focus on the boy, evading her friend's scrutiny. 'Um, you're new here?'

'Yes, I transferred to this university about a month ago.'

'What's your name?' Mariam asked next, wishing to keep the conversation going. It felt oddly exciting to be talking to him.

'I'm Yusuf.' His eyes moved to Sunni. 'And you are?'

'Oh, me? I'm Sunni,' she said, caught off-guard at being brought into the conversation.

Yusuf exchanged a few pleasantries with Sunni but soon turned his attention back to Mariam. 'Where would you like to meet up to work on our assignment?' he asked.

'Um, I don't know. How about one of the small cafés in town?'

'Sounds like a plan,' he said casually.

'Here's my number in case you need to contact me.' Mariam scribbled the digits on a page of her notebook before tearing it out to give to him.

'Thanks.' Yusuf pocketed it. 'I'll see you soon then.'

'Yeah, see you soon,' Mariam echoed softly.

*

'Beta! Beta! Oh my God! Beta, Beta!' Mum yelled.

'What is it?' Mariam asked, rushing down the stairs.

'Who is this?' Mum asked furiously.

'Who's who?'

'You got a missed call from someone called Yusuf!'

'Oh, him,' Mariam shrugged. 'We're working on an assignment together, that's all.'

'Wait. You're hanging out with boys?' Mum looked outraged.

'No. As I said, it's an assignment for class. I don't know why you're making such a big deal out of it.' Mariam turned and went back upstairs to her room. Her mother followed and watched her finish packing her bag with books and a notepad.

'Where do you think you're going now, young lady?'

'I'm going to work on my assignment.'

'You can study in your room. There's no need to go out.'

'No, I'm going out to work on my assignment with Yusuf.' Mariam swung her satchel across her shoulder and headed for the door.

'Are you ignoring me? Come back here right now before I phone your father!'

'Look, Mum, I'm sorry but I have to go.' And Mariam walked out before her mother could make any other threats.

*

Mariam got off the bus and entered the café. She saw Yusuf sitting at the back, sipping his coffee. She smiled and headed for his table. 'Hi, how are you?'

'I'm great, thanks,' Yusuf responded with a bright smile.

'What are you working on?' Mariam asked, eyeing the sketchbook in front of him.

'Nothing,' he said, and flipped the book shut, hiding whatever he had been drawing.

'Didn't look like nothing,' Mariam teased.

'It's just a piece I'm working on.' Yusuf looked defensive.

'No way! You're an artist?'

'Not necessarily. I just doodle in my spare time. Back in Edinburgh, whenever I had free time, I would find a quiet place to draw.' He got up to pay for his coffee and offered to buy her a drink too.

She waited until Yusuf went to the counter, then reached across to pull his sketchbook over. She opened the book and began looking through his artwork. Then, seeing him start to make his return with her drink, Mariam hurriedly closed the pad and pushed it back to his side of the table.

'You know, we could really use something like this for our assignment.' She pointed at his book. 'Think about it. A few pieces of writing alongside some drawings to capture how we view ourselves.'

'You know what? That's not a bad idea.'

They discussed ideas for their assignment and spent some time taking notes. The project was beginning to take shape. Then Mariam's phone vibrated.

'Shoot! My mum's calling me. I have to go now, but let's meet up again the same time next week and continue the assignment.'

'Great,' Yusuf nodded. 'I'll look forward to that.'

*

'What did you guys get up to in the café?' Sunni laid back on Mariam's bed, stretching out her arms and legs.

'Nothing much. We just spoke a little bit and started organizing what we want to do for the assignment.'

'Cool, so nothing else happened?' Sunni couldn't hide her curiosity.

'Of course nothing else happened. Why are you asking?'

'Just interested.' Sunni waved her hand nonchalantly. For a moment there was silence.

Then: 'Okay, so here's what it was like.' Mariam lowered her voice. The two girls chatted away for a few minutes, until Mariam's mum opened the door.

'Mariam, Sunni, dinner's ready. We're all waiting at the table for you.'

'Sorry, Mum, we're coming.' The delicious aroma wafted into her room. 'I'm so hungry. Come on, let's go eat.'

'Auntie-ji, your food smells amazing.' Sunni sniffed the air as she walked into the kitchen.

'Thank you, beta. I made it especially for you.' Mum embraced Sunni.

'Aw, Auntie-ji. You didn't have to.' Sunni hugged her back.

Mariam sighed. Her mum always tried so hard to please her guests with food.

Mariam and Sunni sat down at the table with the rest of the family and tucked into their food.

'How is your family, Sunni?' asked Mariam's stepfather.

'Alhamdulillah, everyone is well,' Sunni replied, on her best behaviour.

'Give your family our salaams, and if you ever need anything, let us know. Okay?'

'Thank you, Uncle-ji. I'll give everyone your salaams.' Sunni got up and kissed Mariam's mother's cheek. 'Thank you for the delicious meal, Auntie-ji.'

'You're going already?' Mariam asked.

'Yes, my mum sent a text saying come home.'

'The next time you come over, stay over.' Mum was loading the dishwasher. 'Oh, here – take some food home for your family.' She handed Sunni some containers full of food.

'Thank you,' Sunni said. 'Okay, salaam everyone. Thanks for having me.'

'Any time, beta,' Mariam's mum said, opening the door to let her out.

'Should we do some more work on this assignment?' Mariam asked.

'All right,' Yusuf said, putting his work on the table.

'Wow! You did all these drawings? They're beautiful.'

'Thanks. Yes, I drew them. I thought they might look good for our portfolio,' Yusuf said shyly.

'Definitely. Your talent is unreal,' Mariam commented, flicking through his drawings in awestruck silence.

'Thanks,' Yusuf repeated. He looked thrilled.

'Well, this is my work so far.' Mariam laid out her pages.

'That's a lot of writing.' Yusuf seemed a bit startled by the reams of paper spread before him.

'I stayed up all night trying to finish it off,' she confided. 'I'm shattered now, but it was worth it.'

'Well, it looks fantastic. I can't wait to read all this.'

'Thank you.' Mariam felt a blush creep over her cheeks.

They took up their work again, chatting to one another in a relaxed way. After a while, Yusuf said, 'I think that's us done: we're ready to give in our assignment.'

'Yeah. Now we just need to pass,' Mariam joked.

'We did a great job. Inshallah, we'll pass.'

'I should probably head home now. I guess I'll see you around,' Mariam said, feeling strangely upset.

Yusuf didn't look upset at all. He gathered up his belongings. 'Yes. See you later.'

*

The next day, Yusuf opened his locker to collect his folders, and an envelope fell out. He picked it up and read the note inside.

Salaam
I was wondering if you want to meet up later? I would
love to see and hear more about your drawings.
From Mariam

Smiling to himself, Yusuf folded the note, pocketing it before hurrying off to the lecture hall, where the lecturer was already addressing the class.

'Good morning, everyone. I'm sure I don't have to remind you that today is the deadline for your submission. If you could all please place your work assignments on my desk.'

'Do you think you'll pass?' Sunni whispered to Mariam, pulling her work out of her bag.

'I hope so. What about you? Do you think you did okay?'

'My partner and I worked pretty hard, so I'm hoping for the best,' Sunni yawned.

'Once you hand in your reports you are free to go to the library and revise for your exams,' the lecturer instructed.

'To the library then?' Sunni tilted her head at Mariam.

'Sorry, I think I'll give it a miss.' Mariam was scanning the room.

'Who are you looking for?'

'Yusuf.'

'Why?'

Mariam didn't answer her as she had just spotted Yusuf making his way out. She hastened after him, calling his name. Catching him up, she asked, 'Do you want to meet up later so you can show me more of your drawings?'

'That'd be fun,' he agreed.

'Great! Let's meet at the same café as last time.' Mariam left with a bounce in her step.

*

'Tell me a bit more about your art,' Mariam invited, lifting the cup of coffee to her lips.

'You know when you find something interesting, or if you have a life-changing experience, you write about it or take photos?' Yusuf began. 'That's what I did through my drawings.'

Mariam frowned. 'How do you mean, a life-changing experience?'

Yusuf went quiet for a moment, before taking a breath. 'Lots of things happened to me before I found Islam,' he admitted. 'The truth is, I come from a family who see no pleasure in equality and simplicity. They aren't very religious. My brothers would always come home drunk and encouraged me to do the same, but I knew that wasn't what I wanted. I was searching for peace and freedom, so I ended up spending most of my time drawing. By the time I was twenty-four, I was thinking of marriage, but seeing my brothers' failed marriages put me off. I never considered finding a girlfriend because most girls in my home town were doing all sorts of stuff: smoking weed, getting drunk, partying all night – the list goes on and on.'

'How did you find Islam?'

'There was this Muslim family in our neighbourhood,' Yusuf shared. 'They never went partying. They were never seen at the pub. They were always very peaceful in their own home and I wondered why. One day I decided to knock on their door and a young man opened it. He shook my hand and welcomed me into his home. He introduced himself as Ismail and said, "Brother, how can I help you?" I warmed to his manners.'

'He does sound really nice.'

'So I told Ismail I wanted to learn about his religion. He invited me to stay for dinner and told me more about Islam. We became very good friends and met regularly. Ismail even invited me to stay over at his place. We went to the masjid together many times, and he showed me how to perform wudu and pray. Although I visited him quite often, I also decided to do my own research. I began reading and learning the Qur'an, hadiths and sunnah. I read Islamic books and watched Islamic lectures. I took my shahada and started attending the masjid a lot more. I realized that there is only one god, Allah, and He is in control of both the heavens and the earth. He is the greatest, the most merciful, and to Him we shall return. My relationship with Allah is the most important and beautiful connection in my life.'

'That's a lovely story. You mentioned you were hoping to get married. Did that ever happen?'

'No, unfortunately I am still single,' Yusuf said with a twinkle in his eye.

'What brought you to this city?'

'Once I told my family I had become a Muslim, they got upset and ordered me to leave their house. I didn't have the money to move to a new city at that time, so for a while I rented another house in the same neighbourhood. I confided in my friend, Ismail, about my situation, and his mother gave him food to bring to me almost every day. She is such a lovely lady.' Yusuf ducked his head, running a hand through his hair. 'Enough about me. Tell me a little bit about you.'

'Oh, my parents come from Pakistan, though I was born here. I have pretty much lived in this city my entire life. My parents got divorced a few years ago. My mum remarried, and I have a younger sister now, as well as an older stepsister and stepbrother. I am also looking into marriage.'

'What about your father? Do you still see him?' Yusuf asked.

'Alhamdulillah, my father is in good health. I visit him whenever I can, and I stay over sometimes,' Mariam replied.

'Alhamdulillah, that's good to hear,' Yusuf said, the corners of his mouth turning up.

*

Two months passed, and Mariam kept in contact with Yusuf, slowly getting to know him. So far, everything she learned about him she liked.

One morning, Mariam went downstairs for breakfast and saw a letter addressed to her on the mat. She opened it up.

Dear Mariam,

Over the past few months, we've really got to know each other, talking about our past life experiences and our interests, as well as what we want to achieve in this life. I enjoy spending time with you. I would like to ask for your hand in marriage. I want to perform a Nikah with you.

If you accept my proposal, meet me at the same café tomorrow at 10 a.m.

Yours truly,

Yusuf

Mariam stared at the letter, butterflies rising in her stomach, not knowing what to think.

'Beta, come and have breakfast,' her mother called.

'Coming, Mum.' Mariam quickly folded the letter and put it in her pocket. She went to the kitchen, helped herself to cereal with milk and sat down at the table.

'How are you, beta?' Mum asked.

'I feel amazing,' Mariam sang out.

'You're certainly in a good mood today.'

'Well, you know, I graduated from uni. How could I not feel amazing?' Mariam said, wolfing down her cereal.

'Beta, you're in no hurry. Why are you rushing your breakfast?' Mum asked.

'I'm off to Sunni's house. We're going on a girls' outing to celebrate,' Mariam explained.

'Oh, how exciting. Have fun.'

'Thanks, Mum. We will.'

*

'Are you interested, then?' Yusuf asked calmly.

Mariam strolled at a leisurely pace beside him through the quiet park.

'Yes, I am, but the thing is, I haven't told my parents yet.' Mariam wrinkled her forehead.

'How come?'

'My mum has high hopes for me to get married to a cousin back in Pakistan. Once Hanna's wedding was out of the way, mum's interest in cousin marriage grew and grew. When she found out that I was working on the assignment with you, she almost had a panic attack. She was freaking out because she thought I was hanging out with boys.'

'Mariam, you do realize I can't ask for your hand in marriage until you speak to them properly?' Yusuf said pointedly.

'I know. Don't worry, I'll speak to them about it. Can I ask you something?'

'Of course.'

'Why me?' Mariam asked, looking at Yusuf.

'We share a lot of interests as well as having some healthy differences, and you seem like a good person. Plus, you said you wanted to move away from the busy lifestyle and live a life more pleasing to God as well as bettering yourself as a Muslim. That's what I'm looking for in a wife: someone who wants to improve her life to please Allah and someone who will be a great companion to spend the rest of my life with.'

'Thank you, I really appreciate it.'

'But what are you looking for in a husband?' Yusuf asked.

'Someone who lives a life of simplicity, who has a good character, who strives to please God in every aspect of his life. Someone who develops the richness of Iman in his heart and the riches of wealth in his hand.'

'Do I meet all those requirements?'

'Yes, in my opinion you do,' Mariam said.

*

'As-salaamu alaykum, Abu-ji, how are you?' Mariam asked upon entering the house.

'Wa alaykum salaam, beta, I am doing fine. How are you?'

'Alhamdulillah, Abu-ji, I am well. Can I make you some chai?'

'Yes, please, that would be lovely.' Abu-ji beamed at his daughter.

Mariam made the tea and brought it into the living room. She sat next to her father and they started chatting.

'Abu-ji, there's something I need to tell you.'

'What is it, beta?' he replied, looking uneasy.

'Someone asked for my hand in marriage.'

'Is he Muslim?' Abu-ji asked.

'Yes, he is, but Mum wants me to marry a cousin back home in Pakistan,' Mariam said.

'Well, if he's a good Muslim, with decent morals and character, then you have my permission to marry him. This is not about what your mum wants, this is about what *you* want and what you think is right for you,' Abu-ji stated firmly.

'Thanks, Abu-ji.' Tears welled in Mariam's eyes as she gave her dad a hug.

'No problem, but just promise me that you will still continue to visit me and stay loyal to me and your mother.'

'Of course I will,' Mariam said. 'But what shall I say to Mum?'

'Don't worry, I will speak to her about it. I promise.'

*

Mariam walked into her house and heard her mum calling from the kitchen table. 'As-salaamu alaykum.'

'Wa alaykum salaam,' Mariam replied. 'Is everyone asleep?'

'Yes, everybody's upstairs sleeping,' Mum replied. 'Your father phoned.'

'He did?' Mariam said nervously.

'Look, beta, you know I only want what's best for you because I care about you and love you very much,' Mum said.

'I know you do, and I love and care about you too,' Mariam said.

'I heard Yusuf asked to get engaged to you.'

'Yes, he did.'

'But wouldn't you much rather marry someone back home?'

'No, I wouldn't,' Mariam replied. 'That's not what I want, that's what you want.'

'So, what do *you* want?' Mariam's mum asked.

'I want to marry someone who's a pious Muslim, with firm morals and a kind personality. Someone who lives their life to seek Allah's pleasure, and someone who will be a good companion and respect me and my family.'

'And does Yusuf fit the bill?' Mum asked.

'Yes, he does. That's why I want to marry him. Give him a chance, Mum,' Mariam pleaded.

'Okay, I'll tell you what. Invite him over for dinner tomorrow,' Mum said.

'Thanks.' Mariam felt a great weight lift from her shoulders.

*

'So? What do you think of Yusuf?' Mariam asked the day after their dinner together.

'Yusuf does seem to live up to your expectations,' Mum said. 'Overall, he seems like a good man.'

'So?' Mariam said.

'As much as I hate saying this, you have my permission to marry him.'

'Really?' Mariam asked.

'Yes, really.'

'Thank you, Mum.' Mariam gave her a hug and rushed for the door.

'Where are you going now?' Mum asked.

'To tell Yusuf the good news, obviously.' Mariam phoned him from her room. They exchanged some pleasantries until Mariam asked him to meet her at the park. She had something to tell him, she said. He promised to be there in ten minutes.

Ten minutes later, Mariam was at the park waiting for Yusuf. She spotted him in the distance and hurried up to meet him.

'It's all worked out,' she said excitedly. 'My mum and dad gave us permission to get married.'

'Really? That's fantastic!'

'I know – I can't believe this is happening,' Mariam gushed.

*

'Are you and Yusuf fully organized for the wedding?' Mum asked nervously.

'Yes, everything's sorted, and my stuff is packed ready for when I move into his house.'

'Beta.'

'Yes, Mum?'

'I'm going to miss you so much.' A tear dropped from Mum's eye.

'I'll miss you too, Mum, please don't cry. I promise to come and visit.' Mariam soothed her mother, and embraced her fondly.

'I know you will, beta. It's just hard to see you go, especially with Hanna married already. I thought you would stick around a little longer,' Mum said, wiping her eyes.

At that moment, Amara ran downstairs and put her arms around her big sister.

'I don't want you to leave,' the younger girl said.

'Why not?' Mariam asked.

'Because I'll never get to see you again,' Amara said.

'That's not true. You're still going to see me, and you can come over and stay during the school holidays.' Mariam cupped the girl's chin.

'Really?'

'Really,' Mariam said firmly.

*

Eight months had passed since Mariam and Yusuf's wedding. One day, Mariam's doorbell rang, and she opened the door to find her mum and little sister standing before her.

'As-salaamu alaykum,' she said, delighted to see them. 'It's been a while. Come in!'

Amara gave Mariam a hug. 'I missed you. It's been so boring at home without you.'

'Aw, I missed you too. Do you want to have a sleepover tonight?'

'Can I, Mum?' Amara asked.

'Yes, as long as you behave.' Mum shot her a stern look.

'I promise I will,' Amara said, jumping up and down with excitement.

Marian led the visitors down the hall to the kitchen, asking, 'Are you guys hungry? I've got some food you can have.'

'Only if you and Yusuf eat with us,' Mum said.

Yusuf walked into the kitchen and greeted them warmly. 'As-salaamu alaykum, how are you both?'

'Wa alaykum salaam, alhamdulillah, we are well. I'm glad to see that you are both happy and living peacefully,' Mum said with a smile.

Everything about their home revealed to her that together, her beloved daughter and son-in-law had created a life of harmony and simplicity, to reflect their natures and the path they had chosen for themselves.

Proper and Perfect?

Zarina Harriri

I can't tell you the exact moment when the tingling started. I just remember watching our semi-naked gardener Brian trimming the hedges, his bare back dripping, gleaming in the scorching sun. That was a day to remember, partly because 22 degrees was a temperature rarely reached in our little seaside town in Scotland. Oh, and that was the first time I had ever felt something in my nether regions for the opposite sex. I was fourteen.

Puberty had hit me hard at thirteen, and my unibrow (amongst other things) grew uncontrollably, almost overnight. Until I finally decided to deal with it using my brother Sufiyan's razor. I ended up taking most of my left brow with it.

Being one of the only minority people in my town, I found high school challenging. My bushy hair and brown skin meant I attracted a lot of attention: mostly negative, of course.

What colour are your nipples, Shaz?

I wonder if her fanny is brown too . . .

Look at how hairy her back is; bet her minge is ten times worse!

Safe to say, my insecurities generated themselves after that.

With hindsight, I realize I was a little late to the party. While most of my peers at the age of sixteen were being fingered, wanked, or having full-on sex, just holding hands caused me a week of restless nights. To be fair, my mother had eyes everywhere. Even if I so much as went out for a quick daytime meal with a boy in my friendship group, she would know before the lunch hour was over. No way was I allowed to stray from her idea of the 'perfect' Muslim daughter.

My South Asian Muslim parents had lived in Kingsbarn for more than twenty years. How liberal had they become? To be honest, not very. While most of my white peers were being guided through the complicated process of puberty, my mother simply handed me a sanitary towel the first time I bled, saying, 'Here, this will soak it up.'

I used to think the topic of puberty wasn't discussed because it was taboo. But our lack of conversation on the subject, and my inability to approach my mother about it, made me feel that she was just being irresponsible and using sharam or modesty as a way to avoid having difficult discussions.

At home, the related topic of sex was avoided like the coronavirus. On TV, whenever a man or woman even so much as looked at each other with desire, we were told to turn away. If the couple touched, my mother snatched the remote control from our grasp to change the channel and, if the scene was really graphic, our television would be switched off for the rest of the night. I always knew it was supposed to be a deterrent, a way for our parents to control our exposure to the embraces of men and women, women and women, men and men. Hell! Even human—object relations! But all these restrictions did was make me more curious and eager to see and get involved in what my parents were protecting us from.

It was just Sufiyan and me left at home with Mum and Dad. Our two older brothers had moved out soon after they were married. I think my oldest sister-in-law Aisha's midnight moans and groans were part of the reason my parents had encouraged her and my brother to find their own place. This prompted Aisha to blurt out: 'Oh, is this because I'm too loud?'

Now, this was something she should never have acknowledged, let alone said out loud. In fact, Mummy dearest embarrassedly pointed this out: 'Aisha, we were all happier pretending we hadn't heard anything.'

The relationship between my parents had always puzzled me. Our father was a silent but domineering man, six foot two, with a broad build and a slim, square face. Our mother by comparison was a short, plump, rosy-cheeked woman barely reaching my father's shoulders. However, she assured us she had always been his perfect match. In her actions, she was at his beck and call day and night for whatever he needed. In her appearance, she regularly had herself groomed for his admiration, but sadly to cricket sounds and no compliments from him. While in our company, he was fairly passive and indifferent towards her. I used to wonder if the passage of time had caused him to cease displays of affection, or if he really just viewed their relationship as part of his routine.

Sunday and Wednesday evenings were our mum and dad's 'alone time'. On those nights, one and then the other would slink off to their shared room at around eight. Before they went, each parent would encourage my brother and me to keep busy with study, or entertain ourselves with a puzzle or a television show. It was known that this time was not to be disturbed, and their room and the corridor leading up to it were strictly off-limits.

I also found that on the odd Friday, when Sufiyan and I would return home early from school, we would be greeted by a deathly silence in the house, apart from a few faint groans and bangs emanating from upstairs. To signal the news of our arrival to our parents, we would slam the front door behind us. Sure enough, we would then hear muffled sounds of rushing. Soon we'd be met by our father meekly making his way downstairs, followed by our mother looking dishevelled and even rosier than usual.

Our mother was a domineering woman in her own right, fiercely house-proud, very well put-together, kind and hospitable but unapologetically honest. She was obsessed with maintaining my thick dark hair, while I insisted on having it thinned out by the hairdresser. She constantly nagged me to keep my skin out of any type of sunlight, because the whiter the better – apparently. Oh! And I was constantly berated for the nose that 'definitely came from Great-aunt Rubena'. She was good at giving people credit where she felt it was due, but she also enjoyed her drama – both on and off the screen. My days under her rule were spent cleaning, cooking and learning the 'proper' etiquette befitting the perfect Pakistani lady she expected me to be. She took particular pains to ensure I spent my Saturdays becoming intimately acquainted with Henry, our hoover, and of course the highly respected Mr Muscle.

Our parents were focused on our education to the expense of all else. So the days before my acceptance letter for university arrived were some of the most nerve-racking of my life. I had always been a high achiever, so medical school was expected of me. But being accepted almost three hundred miles away in Manchester was definitely not what my mother had anticipated nor what she had hoped for.

'Why has Allah chosen to take you away from me? Why do you have to go so far, beta! I cannot allow you to go,' she shrieked, slumping over the breakfast table and sobbing profusely.

My father, on the other hand, seemed unfazed that I would go to university so far away. 'My beti, the heart surgeon,' he said proudly. He pulled me towards him and enveloped me in his arms. 'I always knew you would do it. My little genius!'

This overwhelmingly positive reaction startled me. I knew my father to be a man of few words and mostly indifferent to what was going on around him. This was the most emotional outburst I had ever witnessed from him, and I loved it. Nevertheless, I couldn't guarantee that cardiology would be my specialty. I hadn't even seen the campus yet, let alone decided what I would do for the rest of my life.

It took many hours of convincing and reassurance, but my mother eventually came around to the idea of me leaving. She was scarred by her friend Zahida's experience. Her son had left for university only to be 'lured' (Zahida's word, not mine) into having sex with a Caucasian girl. This girl ended up pregnant and had 'ruined his life'. I was angered by this double standard. I wanted to scold my mother and assure her that he didn't just fall into the girl's vagina, dick first. But I kept this thought to myself.

Before leaving, my mother coerced me into promising, for the sake of her peace of mind, that I wouldn't take drugs, drink alcohol or fornicate. I did promise, but with my fingers crossed behind me.

My parents dropped me off, and my mother wept again as she left me in my unfamiliar new environment among strangers. It was the first day of Freshers' Week, and the music was already blaring from the common areas, the messy embrace of student life greeting me warmly. I was sharing an annexe with four girls; Yu Yan, Ammarah, Ebi and Suzanne. All were studying for professional qualifications and they all came from big cities in the south of England. When Mum realized I was staying with Ammarah, a five foot six, bright-eyed, slim aspiring Muslim dentist, she was thrilled.

'She looks after herself – she is beautiful,' she beamed. 'I am so glad you will have some Islamic influence around you. You two girls can pray together.'

If I'm honest, I saw Ammarah's religion as a hindrance. I didn't want someone to be watching my every move and judging me for my actions. I didn't want to have to be careful if I decided to bring a boy back to my room. Not that I thought I would do that, but I yearned to be unapologetically reckless and, most of all, free.

It didn't take us flatmates long to get acquainted with each other. Yu Yan was from a very wealthy family whose idea of a congratulatory gift was a bottle of vintage red wine. And so, even though I had assured my mother I would never touch the devil's nectar, I felt it would have been rude not to accept a glass. The wine went straight to my head and the next thing I remember was being at the Student Union in a dress that would have been perfect for the bedroom but was definitely not 'proper' for a young Pakistani woman like myself.

I loved how diverse the population was in Manchester. From the moment of my arrival, I was excited by the idea of meeting so many different types of men from various backgrounds and with contrasting worldviews.

My mum had always made sure I was well versed in Pakistani and Indian musical culture. My love of music and dance came from her and had been nurtured from a young age. As I grew older, there was no musical genre I didn't enjoy. So in my hazy state at the Union that first night, I grabbed Ebi and made sure a space was cleared for us on the dance floor.

Ebi was a deep chocolate brown, tall and curvaceous; I was pretty sure her ass could stop a war. In comparison, I was a medium-built girl with mangoes for breasts and a pancake arse. So you can imagine my surprise when I felt someone brush up against my buttocks. I kept dancing, assuming it was a mistake. Calvin Harris was blaring through the speakers and I could see through the windows the sun beginning to set, the evening light shining directly into my eyes.

The man came closer and put his hands on my barely existing hips. I could feel something throbbing against me, and his touch made me moist as I felt myself burning up. I was almost afraid to look behind me. It was as if by acknowledging his touch I would need to pull myself away from his grasp, the expected 'proper' thing to do. Instead, I backed up into his grip, tugged his hands around my waist and started to roll my hips, as I had done many times at the tame henna parties back home. I looked over my shoulder to face him. He was Chinese; his jaw was square and his build was broad. I had always known I liked white men, but Chinese? This was new. It was probably because my home town was more John and Bob than Chung Lee and Siew Kee.

I embraced the moment, living the way I knew I was supposed to, free and heedless as to what was expected of me.

I am sure I was plied with more nectar, because I can hardly remember getting home. Thankfully, I woke up alone in my bedroom, half-naked and surrounded by a few takeaway containers and bottles of water. Once I plucked up the courage to drag myself out of my room, I found Suzanne lounging on the sofa in the living area. Suzanne was from Yorkshire; her eyes were bright blue and her hair was a rich auburn. She was also starting Medicine and was already well schooled in alcohol and its effects. Consequently, she was full of energy, drinking her coffee and reading Tolstoy, waiting for the rest of us to return from the student version of Narnia.

I was relieved when Suzanne told me that I had spent most of the night dancing with the girls, apart from the short time when Ryan, the handsome Chinese guy, had stolen me away. He had left his number in my phone, she informed me. I thought I had lost my phone – until it was retrieved from the kitchen sink. My heart sank when I saw the twelve missed calls from my mother. In my current state, it was more sensible to just send her a text.

As salaamu alaykum, Mummy, sorry I missed your call. Hope you and Dad got home okay. Just on my way to Freshers' Fair. Speak later, love you!

Ebi, Yu Yan and Ammarah straggled into the common area one by one, looking the worse for wear but ready to recharge with free pizza at the Freshers' Fair.

The fair was spread across numerous halls in the university sports centre. I decided to wander off by myself while the girls gorged on pizza and collected their stationery for the year ahead. I was at the Greenpeace stall when I heard my name.

'Shazia! Shall we go and look for the Islamic Society?' Ammarah enquired, chomping on a slice of non-halal chicken and mushroom pizza.

By this point, I was well aware that people pick and choose what parts of religion they decide to follow, but surely approaching ISOC eating a blatantly haram pizza slice was going a bit far?

'Erm, okay, but I don't want to be forced into joining. I'd prefer not to be known by other Muslims if I'm going out drinking and messing around, Ammarah.'

'What? Are you serious? Most of the ISOC guys are out every weekend! Bet they finish their classes, read Jummah – and then get their drinks in for the Friday-night session they're planning. Don't worry so much.'

We approached the ISOC stand, where there were four student representatives, two women and two men. The stand was beautifully decorated and provided information on a variety of topics. These ranged from fortnightly lectures on Islamic principles such as charity and prayer to personal support for students dealing with issues including anxiety, depression and even alcoholism. I gave them my email address, made small talk about being Scottish in England, took a picture of the stall to send to my mother, and semi-promised them I would make it to their next meeting. I felt keeping it brief would be the best way to maintain my clean-cut, perfect image.

Ammarah already knew one of the guys at the stall. She had started speaking with him on an online forum when she was accepted at the university's dental school.

'You know the guy on the right? That's Bashir – he is in his second year of dentistry. I'm going to marry him one day.' Ammarah sighed lustfully, a twinkle in her eye.

Much of the day passed while I still had heavy brain fog. My body was tired and I could only process what was going on around me from about 8 p.m. I sent my mum the picture of me at the ISOC stall. She seemed satisfied, so I knew I had bought myself another night of freedom from family calls, texts and general bother. She sent me a text.

Well done beti. Have good time. Love to you too.

I wandered into the bathroom, took a shower and got ready to head out with the girls. Just then, Yu Yan burst in excitedly.

'It's toga night, Shazia! I have spare sheets if you need them – Egyptian cotton. My mum packed me some extras. She knows how difficult I find it, doing the laundry.'

'Oh! Yeah, that would be great. Could you help me dress up though? I've never worn a toga before.'

'Of course. I think we'd be best making your toga long though. I wouldn't want someone else trying to feel you up while you are dancing. That Ryan was all over you!'

How could I have admitted that the shorter the toga the better, that I desired to have my legs on show, to be lustfully gazed upon, and maybe even (if my mood allowed) to be touched. This wasn't the perfect image I knew I should portray, so instead I expressed my gratitude.

'Thanks, Yu, you're the best.'

I had accepted that alcohol was an easy way to bond and meet new people and so I allowed myself to dabble. Much of the evening passed in a blur and I had little contact with the many men I came across. Ammarah was the lucky one that evening. She had been grinding on an olive-skinned Italian guy and had disappeared halfway through the night.

I was rudely awoken the next morning by Ammarah's guttural groans. For someone who had never had sex but occasionally watched porn, I felt I had had my fair share in this lifetime of hearing others' breathless cries.

'Faster, faster! Ohhh, deep. Yes, get in me deeper . . . *Ye-es!*'

The squeaks of the cheap metal bedframes we were given filled brief pauses between the moans and slapping sounds. My loins were heating up. I felt slightly perverted as I followed the ordeal like a football match. Climax was reached after approximately seven minutes. Ammarah's friend's gorilla groan caused a sharp but comforting tingle, which prompted me to place my fingers in my labia. The orgasm was followed by Ammarah's incessant giggling and her eventual departure for a shower. I decided that it was best to ignore the pulsating feelings in my clitoris and get up for breakfast.

While I was making a much-needed coffee, Ammarah's friend entered the kitchen in his boxers. My mouth dropped open as I realized he was almost naked and bore a striking resemblance to Michelangelo's David, though with a much more generous package.

'Oh, sorry! I thought there was no one in here . . . I'm Stefan.'

My face burned bright red. It was my own fault, I couldn't tear my eyes away from his crotch. I eventually replied, stuttering, 'I-i-it's okay, I was just leaving. There's plenty of coffee and milk in the fridge.'

Then I rushed back to my room, almost spilling my coffee all over my desk. I pulled off my pyjamas and lay back on my bed, starting to rub, rub, rub.

Ammarah ended up seeing Stefan for a couple of months, and I was lucky enough to bump into him several times during their illicit affair. I remember being so absorbed in my phone after my classes one afternoon that I walked straight into his strong chest. I might have held on to him for a little longer than I should have, but he didn't pull away. That evening, I masturbated until I finally fell asleep from exhaustion. I had learned how to please myself, with Stefan being the perfect stimulus. I felt quite satisfied as I settled into my new regime.

The weeks passed, however, and I saw less and less of Stefan. I had become inundated with coursework and classes. The university schedule was packed tight and I fell into a mundane pattern. The cooking every night and cleaning every weekend that I'd done at home were a distant memory, and unless the girls asked, I rarely made any elaborate meals. Scrambled eggs and toast were my staple dish – desi-style, of course.

There were more than four hundred students on my first year of the course and I found that every day I would meet someone new. As the weeks flew by, this became more of a formality than a novelty. That is, until I met *him*.

I didn't notice him; he saw me. I later discovered that he had seen me as soon as I walked into the first workshop. Maybe it was my slumped posture, or my bright yellow backpack. He said it was the hair, the dark curly strands that he wanted to run his hands through. He approached me and asked if he could take the seat next to me. I looked up at him and was instantly enraptured by his eyes. The deep green was mesmerizing, set against his dark skin. My heart jumped a beat, time stood still and sound fuzzed up.

His name was Devon and he came from south London. When he was only fifteen, his mother had died from ovarian cancer. It was then he decided that Medicine was his calling. His upbringing hadn't been easy. He was the oldest of six children from a working-class Caribbean family and had taken a part-time job from the age of twelve. He had the drive that was the making of powerful men. I could see he had known much pain and little joy. I knew that by comparison, my life had been easy. But he saw the weight of expectations on my shoulders, the perfect image I struggled to maintain. He could sense my trials and their effects when he first met me. It was his way with words that really appealed: how he could describe the driest topic with exuberance but in depth. This was why I let myself fall.

We spent most of our evenings together, usually studying or speaking about our home lives and our passions. As our relationship progressed, our evenings would end with us cuddling, usually in his single bed but sometimes in mine. I used to lie awake listening to Devon's deep breathing, trying to make peace with my actions. I was also trying to reconcile myself to my mother's expectations, which I had found so hard to live by. Devon never pushed me to be intimate with him. We would indulge in foreplay, a kiss here and a lick there, but only when I allowed myself.

It was the last Thursday of the winter term. I had finished for the day and knew Devon would be home, so I called ahead and made my way over to his place. It had been a long time coming and I couldn't resist the temptation any longer. The feeling was unlike anything I had ever experienced before.

I entered his room where he was waiting on the edge of his bed, legs open, watching me with his beautiful soul-baring eyes. I gazed at him, biting my lip. I felt as though his crotch was calling out, inviting me to come and rest myself on top. I had been dancing around the idea of intercourse for long enough. Although Devon had never expected anything, I knew I no longer wanted to fight against my affinity for him.

I know I should have acted 'proper'. That said, if I was the one to fulfil his desire, then surely this would make me perfect?

Acid Reflux

Afshan D'souza-Lodhi

For Aisha's parents, the matter of their daughter's wellbeing after the terrible incident came second to the all-important question: 'What will people say?'

Discussing further options with doctors in the Accident & Emergency Department of the hospital left them learning new phrases – like skin grafts, skin depigmentation, septicaemia and renal failure. They hadn't even begun to talk about possible psychological effects when Aisha started to regain consciousness. As doctors informed her of her condition, she kept what remained of her mouth slightly ajar and looked at them calmly, her left hand constantly pushing the button by her side.

The assessments began shortly afterwards.

*

Once she was back home, going out became a problem. No matter how small the family function, Aisha and her mother would try on at least five different outfits before coming downstairs. There had been a time in the past when finding the suit that made them look at once slim, fashionable, classy and modest had been a priority. Now it was a different story. Colours, fashion, quality of stitching were all traded in for length and concealment.

Aisha's mother Shahida looked her daughter up and down then tutted, saying, 'It doesn't cover enough of your neck. You can see . . . everything.'

She meant ugly, shrivelled skin.

Again, Aisha began to look in her closet of browns and blacks and pretended she was contemplating an alternative outfit.

'Do I even have to go?' she asked.

'What do you mean, do you even have to go? They called us and asked about you. You *have* to go. And do something about your hair. Wear that wig I got you.'

Shahida thought this would make her daughter's problems go away. Her hair was growing back, but every time it grew to an acceptable length, some infection or another flared up and it was shaved off. And short hair on an Asian woman? No. Fake hair could be used to cover up much of the damage. What exactly it would be protecting was another question entirely. They both knew it wasn't modesty.

'I may as well wear a hijab again, Mum.'

'So that your face will stand out more? What is it you want from me, huh? You want everyone to see your face and ask? Allah only knows what I have done to deserve this.' She started rambling on in a mix of Urdu and Punjabi, and Aisha tuned out.

She finally picked up the wig, sighing, 'Fine. I'll wear it. '

Years of car journey discussions that were once dominated by her father were now filled with empty lectures. Aisha had to give it to him. He did try.

'Aisha beta, you look nice.'

'What do you mean, she looks nice?' her mother interrupted. 'Of course she looks nice. Did I not dress her? If I'd left her to dress herself, she'd look like a jungli or something.'

Aisha knew better than to argue. Any attempt at a conversation would be shot down by her mother's reflected stare in the rear-view mirror. This was often followed by her turning round to shoot another look, one that prompted Aisha to adjust her dupatta. Behold: the real reason her mother didn't drive.

Today Aisha was in the mood for games. For the first time in a long while, she didn't lower her gaze respectfully. She stared back at her mother's reflection and tried a puzzled expression. She attempted to furrow already furrowed skin and tilted her head to one side. Her mother's fixed look became a frown and it pierced.

It was her parents who breathed deeply before bracing themselves to ring the doorbell. Aisha herself just stood there, counting the petals on a half-closed daisy.

Once inside, having avoided being the topic of conversation but not the centre of every stare, Aisha decided she'd try to speak to one of the girls gawping at her. Time to make someone else uncomfortable. She walked up to a girl who was holding a glass of the pink stuff – non-alcoholic but nursed by the aunties there like one does mulled wine – and sat down next to her.

'Hello.'

'Hi.'

'I'm Aisha.' She looked at her victim expectantly, her hand held out ready for shaking.

'I'm Sophia.'

Sophia looked at her. Like *really* looked at her. This was something Aisha was not used to. People didn't look at her. They looked through her or gazed down, silently apologizing to her. Those who did look would become embarrassed within seconds. Only children would feast their eyes. That is, until mindful parents told them it was rude to stare at ugly brown women.

But Sophia looked at her. Stared, actually. And it was a *fuck me* not a *fuck you*. A *fuck me, you're interesting*.

'Your face, I mean. Sorry, I . . .'

Aisha didn't give her a chance to fully apologize. 'It's acid burns,' she interrupted.

'Oh.' Sophia missed a beat. Then: 'What happened?'

'My makeup remover wouldn't work.'

Sophia paused, waited for some sort of continuation from Aisha. When none came, she smiled, and soon both were giggling loudly.

Sophia stopped and watched as this strange girl shook with laughter. Her eyes squinted and loose skin pulled taut on one side while gathering on the other. Her face was wrinkled and transparent, and the blood vessels were noticeable beneath the skin. On one side of her mouth, there were no lips to speak of, just a down-turned wound where the face ended to make room for the mouth. She must have been fair and lovely once. Now when she laughed her eyelashes only half stained her cheekbones.

Sophia studied how her new friend's face lacked grace and gravitas when she laughed. Yet there was something very graceful about the way she threw her head back, her dupatta slipping to reveal more wrinkled skin. For a moment she wondered how far down the burns went. Did they cross over her nipples? Or did they leave a respectful area of clean skin around the areola? What was left of her nipples, in fact? Were they completely burnt? Were they called burns? These were questions that would have to wait till later.

Half the room had turned their heads looking at the pair. A woman, she guessed it was Aisha's mother, gave them the what-the-hell-do-you-think-you're-doing stare. It didn't bother Aisha. She just slurped her chai and moved the half of her face that she could into what looked like a sly smile.

The conversation turned. Sophia forgot about her many questions as she thought of something more pressing.

'Do you have Twitter?' She took her phone out in anticipation.

For the first time that night, Aisha felt uncomfortable. 'Erm. Yes.'

'What's your @?'

'Aisha Siddiqui.' Sensing that Sophia would ask about the spelling of her username, Aisha took the phone and found herself, saying, 'Here, let me.'

Instead of technology monopolizing the conversation, it opened it up. They talked about favourite poems and recited couplets and one-liners. At one point, Sophia was quoting Shakespeare. Or at least Aisha thought she was. It could have been gibberish laced with thees, thous and thuses. It didn't matter. Blagging was an art, after all, and one that Aisha appreciated very much.

Sophia, who had her phone out for the entirety of the conversation, kept looking down at it.

'Am I not interesting enough?' Aisha enquired.

'No. It's not that. It's just . . .'

'What, waiting for your boyfriend to text back? Or girlfriend?'

Sophia's head shot up at the word 'girlfriend'. The expression she wore was not one of shock or disgust, but rather of surprise. Surprise at the acceptance which had come so casually.

'Neither. I want to take a picture, that's all. I'm a little sentimental like that. May I? Would you be the subject?'

'I don't know. Shall I?'

'May I?' Sophia held up her phone.

'You may.' Aisha tilted her head. 'Which side do you want? I must warn you, my right side is my bad side. It's a bit rebellious that way.'

A few selfies later and the pair were forced to end their conversation. Unlike most parents who got up, said their goodbyes and then hovered near the door for hours, Aisha's parents had a habit of leaving promptly.

'I'll see you online,' Aisha said, and winked at Sophia before getting up and joining her parents, who were amazed that their daughter had actually made a friend. And a normal-looking one at that.

*

The drive home was filled with smiles from everyone. There were no stares from the rear-view mirror. Not until her mother turned to the back of the car and said, 'It's nice you made a friend, Aisha beta. Who is she? Is she Malaysia wali bhaji's daughter?'

Malaysia wali bhaji had a name. Not that anyone ever remembered it.

'I think so.'

'She called Sophie?'

'Sophia,' Aisha snapped at her mother and pulled off her wig and the sock cap in one swift movement. Sophia was hers.

But Shahida wasn't giving up. 'What does she do?'

'I dunno.'

'You chatted to her for so long and didn't ask what she does? Maybe she'll be able to motivate you to do something with *your* life. And next time don't be so loud. Everyone was looking at you.'

And it had been going so well. Luckily Aisha didn't have to bear any more, for the car was about to turn onto their street.

*

Hey Aisha, it's me, Sophisticated. You okay? Wanted to know if you were free next week to grab a drink or something? X

Sophia, not sophisticated. New phone hasn't learnt my name yet. X

Hi, yeh what day? How d'ya get my numba? nd autocorrect mistakes are always fun :)

Facebook. You don't mind, do you? How does Saturday sound? X

Nah, its cool. Thought I'd kept it on private. Arvo?

What's arvo? Haha! Facebook and privacy. That's hilarious X

Afternoon! nythin intrestin planned?

I have. But if I told you I'd have to kill you! Pick you up at yours 1pm OK? X

what u found ma address on fb 2?

No your mum gave it mine.

*

A circus. Sophia had found some discounted tickets in one of those shops that seemed to have more electronics on offer than they could keep on display. Now they were driving. Or rather, Sophia was driving. With only one fully-functioning eye, driving would have been a risky job for Aisha. Not to mention that she didn't have a driving licence. She rarely went out.

Nervousness and angst began to set in. Sophia was beautiful, conventionally so, but Aisha had managed to get a brief glimpse into her soul, enough to know that it was beautiful too. Sophia was probably blessed with a winning personality, intelligent brain *and* beauty: the great trifecta. All Aisha had to offer was comedy through trying not to dribble as she drank pink tea. And now they were on their way to the circus. Historically a place where disfigured people were put on display for 'normal' people. Was Sophia trying to say something by taking her there?

Sophia switched on the music player and M.I.A.'s 'Bad Girls' reverberated through the car. Aisha attempted to lip sync to the song.

'I love this song,' she said.

'I know.'

'You know?'

'Well, I guessed.'

'Bad Girls' carried on.

Aisha caught her reflection in the mirror and did the usual mandatory inspection of her face. She rubbed with vigour at a small smudge of black under her jawline. Without any encouragement she started explaining.

'It's kala tikka. My mother. Er, she . . . it's to ward off . . .'

'Aisha, I know what kala tikka is.'

'Right.'

*

They sat in a bar to kill time. More specifically to burn an hour. Sophia watched as Aisha picked up her drink, her eyes meeting those of the girl behind the bar, who had a nose-piercing and strange-coloured hair. Aisha did not look away, and the girl seemed to be hypnotized, a terrified, limp smile hovering over her round face. Unblinking, Aisha lifted the gin and tonic to her lips and took a long sip, which caused an ugly dribble to leak out of the side of her destroyed mouth.

She knew what the bar girl was thinking. She wanted to ask Aisha if she needed a straw but didn't dare. She didn't know which option was polite. Was it polite to make allowances for differences, or was it polite to ignore them until they were pointed out to you – as if you could ignore that face? The bar girl was paralysed by social uncertainty.

*

It was in a car park, of all places. The car park beside the stadium in which clowns and acrobats were throwing themselves around. At least it was underground. The circus would have to wait for another day. Their hands fumbled and Aisha pushed her partner against the back of the driver's seat. This was supposed to be passionate. Instead it was verging on aggressive.

Sophia winced. She tried not to show pain, instead focusing on getting her lips back on Aisha's. She was still uncertain about what her partner's lips felt like. Kissing puckered skin and trying to find lips that should have been there proved rather difficult.

Noses clashed on her first attempt. Aisha moved her head the same way as Sophia's and instead of their faces neatly tucking into each other's as in the movies, their chins met. Aisha, not willing to give up just yet, continued her ministrations lower down. Collar bones: a safer seduction point. The noise of cars and lights catching them made her hit Sophia's chin, causing blood to draw from the woman's lip. While Sophia plastered her lip with a little saliva, Aisha adjusted her clothes and sat up straight in the car.

They sat in silence for what felt like hours. Time does that at awkward moments.

Sophia broke the silence first. 'Your face. What actually happened?'

Aisha wasn't sure how to respond. She'd scrolled right past the Buzzfeed article that in meme form had provided a step-by-step guide on how to talk to your potential date about past trauma.

'Some ISIS wannabe killed some white people, and a bunch of blokes here needed someone, some*thing* to blame.'

Sophia cocked her head, hoping for a more detailed response. 'That's it?'

'I was a hijabi.'

'You talk in poetry.'

'It wasn't poetic.'

'I meant . . .'

'I know.'

*

Sophia's flat was far away from any loud or sudden noises. At first, they sat on the bed making idle conversation. It was hard to talk about anything once you'd opened the box to past trauma. Maybe this was why people didn't talk about bad memories. Both knew the reason they were there, it was just a case of who made the first move.

Sophia did – she was proving to be the instigator in their relationship. She even managed to convince her partner that the laptop should record them. They were both fired up, and yet Sophia loved in English – a distant, vanilla sort of love. Instead of loving being a freeing and risky emotion, between them it was becoming almost stifling. Nevertheless, Aisha persisted. Fighting awkward touches with soft caresses and trying to soothe sensitive skin with her tongue, she attempted to finish this ordeal. Finally, the two of them lay heaving, face up on the bed.

Aisha rang her mother and between 'salaams' and 'yes, Mums', she lied about having a movie night with Sophia. This mendacity was a skill most girls living under no-privacy roofs have learned by the age of ten.

*

Sophia left to shower. For Aisha, there was something about a few hours of almost-passion that didn't warrant a shower, despite excessive sweating.

She found herself looking through her *lover*'s laptop as her *friend* (maybe that was a better word) scrubbed clean. Having found a decent track to hum along to, she grew bored and decided to do a little snooping. She opened folders and files, hoping to find something entertaining.

Jackpot! The folder contained photos. Each image told a different story, not about the subject but the photographer. Sophia had talent. Aisha spent a few seconds on each picture and occasionally backtracked while she tried to understand this new friend she had made.

It was very rare for Aisha to see herself in photos. Her mother insisted that the burns not be documented until they were healed enough to be unnoticeable.

So when Aisha started flicking through the images that Sophia had taken of her, she didn't immediately recognize herself. The angles of her face in the images showed a beauty that Aisha had never associated with herself. Her face was art. With each click a new image, a new perspective, a new world was thrown upon Aisha. As she looked at every photo, she fell more deeply in love with herself, and in turn the photographer.

For someone to see such beauty in *her* face, for them to be able to capture it, make it hold ninety-nine words with each image – this was what romance was about. Not rolling around in bed for hours failing to come to a climax.

*

Sophia didn't walk back into her room but stumbled in awkwardly to find Aisha staring intently at the screen. Aisha looked up in time to find her barely towel-covered lover (yes, she was definitely *lover*-worthy) catching her eye.

In a moment of perfect synchronization, they stilled. Just looking at each other. Just eyes meeting eyes.

Neither of them felt the need to say or do anything rash. There was no need to say anything other than what needed to be whispered.

A few seconds passed and, at exactly the same moment, they looked away.

Love Letter

Shelina Janmohamed

When I told you that I was writing this story for you, you giggled. I asked if you were laughing because you thought it was a funny idea, or because you were pleased that I have chosen to write about you. Maybe you've inherited my own giggle, this laughter that shakes your body uproariously when something makes you happy.

I remember holding you next to my skin after you were born. You were mine. A small creature that I wanted to hold for ever. You're eight already, and here I am still trying to work out how to be a good mother. I thought I had womanhood all figured out until I became a mum. Now I am trying to understand how to be me, at the same time as helping you to be you. I was told that motherhood is always about putting your children first, that it's all about you – but I've found that's not quite true. You need me to be who I am, so you can watch, and learn, and experiment, and work out how to be you.

I see so much of myself in you. The way you look. The way you think. The way you see patterns in unconnected things and find meaning in them. You puzzle about the way the world is, but do you wonder about your place in it as much as I do?

I have all the worries mums usually have. Schools, and universities, employment and security, good friends, and health, protection from bad choices and bad people. And love. I hope that you'll find love. Because love is everything for Muslims. Love and justice and compassion.

The world feels lacking in all of those at the moment. And it is in particularly short supply for you, because you are female, and because you are from a Muslim family. I haven't told you this yet – I don't want to. Instead, I am working on painting your dreams with you, your vision of how wondrous this world could be, and the extraordinary experiences you could have within it. That's how I can prevent you from becoming fearful of the world. I want you to know that you have a place in it, and that it is your right to be in it. I want you to know that it is your right to enjoy it.

Yes, I want love for you, for love is a many-splendoured thing.

Love in your family home.

Love for friends and community.

Love for the One who created you, and who put the Divine Spark in you.

Love for a husband who will bask in how exquisite you are, a husband who will help you sparkle.

I want all of these things for you, but I also want you to shape your own story. As a Muslim woman I wish you to know that all of these are in your gift, and you can decide. One day I will share my hope with you that you will always turn your compass to the Divine light. Because that is where I believe you will find Love, the love that really matters.

Giving advice in this way is what all mothers do, yet even as I write this, knowing that others will read it, I worry that I'll be accused of forcing you to believe. Of telling you how to live your life. Of oppressing you, when all I want is to share with you what I have learned, and walk with you on a path I believe will make you happy and which will ensure that the world is a better place because you are in it. I want to walk on that path with you for as long as I can, but as you grow up, you will be the one leading, and I will be a voice in your ear. The choices are yours, but you will hear my words, and I want those words to matter.

I'm not teaching you to be me, I'm teaching you to be yourself. The poet Khalil Gibran tells parents about their children: 'You may give them your love but not your thoughts, for they have their own thoughts. You may house their bodies but not their souls, for their souls dwell in the house of tomorrow.'

I want to watch your tomorrow and find out who you will become, because you delight me with the way you think and your ideas about the world and the way you are negotiating your place within it.

How do I tell you that being married is a wonderful thing? The soft embrace of a man, his warmth and safety. His belief and encouragement. His companionship and his gentle correction of your mistakes so you can do better. His support in facing head-on the difficulties that life will inevitably bring, so you can emerge through the storms rather than be crushed by them. How can I tell you about this kind of love, of which people so rarely speak? I don't mean falling in love, I don't mean being Layla and finding your Majnun as in the old Arabic story. I mean a kind of love in which your innermost self can emerge, in which its prickly edges can be smoothed and its shine polished.

I'm conscious that whenever we talk about love and marriage, about womanhood and humanity, that my book is on the shelf. That book in which I wrote about love and marriage and desire. That book where my secrets were shared with so many women in so many countries. That book which has prompted a thousand messages to me about how it affected those women, and men too.

But what will that book mean to you? How can a daughter make sense of her mother's longing for love and romance, for fulfilment and intimacy?

When you were at nursery, all the children and teachers wanted to be your best friend. You have a positive energy that is glorious to be around. It is calm and inviting, but not imposing. It is happy in itself and reaches out to others without feeling the need to change itself or force itself. I remember the little boys used to love you in particular. A small gaggle of them would follow you around. Will it be the same as you get older?

I'm excited to know what love will mean to you. I'm excited that love may kiss you on the lips and awaken your soul. I don't feel jealous of the man who will trigger those emotions in you. Why would I? I want you to experience those things. From afar, I will be cheering you both on. All I can do is help you be ready for him, to learn how to ride the waves of feelings.

In your search for love, you may well declare that you want marriage and children, to have one man, and to be in a structured relationship. However, that may seem staid and old-fashioned by the time you grow up. To find someone like-minded, and to shape your lives and stay together could present new challenges in a future unknown.

There was always a rhythm to life when I was growing up, a natural order, and a traditional way in which things had always been done. But that rhythm seems to have been broken. I have some responsibility for breaking it too, for I did something different and now we have to tread new pathways.

I wonder how you will find someone, and whether I will have a role in that. How will your father and I check he is good enough for you and trust him to fulfil you? I wonder what he will be like, mostly because I know that what parents imagine isn't always what our children want. Is it terribly stuffy of me to ask that we like him too, and that our hearts are gladdened when we think of him with you?

It's natural that traditions change over time, especially when communities move across the world. Add to that the fact that the culture of relationships has also transformed dramatically within this period. I can't help but wonder if you've missed something by not being steeped in those traditions of marriage that I was brought up with. They do offer some structure within which to find yourself, and contain parameters that at least acknowledge the value of a relationship. But you are *you*: you have to have your own experiences. And the whole point of my going through them was so that you don't have to.

Let me speak frankly. So many of those ideas and traditions were frustrating; so many were, in fact, mind-bogglingly idiotic. So many were designed to make women feel bad and keep them in an inferior place – and yet the whole system was nonetheless propped up *by* women. What will you find yourself struggling against?

You are my child and I am your mother. When I open up and tell you about love and desire, this will reveal to you my imperfections. But I will make myself vulnerable to you. Whatever you ask me I will answer you, about love and relationships and intimacy and desire. Because love is at the centre of who you are as a Muslim.

However, I'm also worried about your future as a Muslim girl. The dark clouds of anti-Muslim hatred have been gathering like a storm about to burst. Muslim women bear the brunt of it; we are targets in the crosshairs of misogyny and Islamophobia, and as you are of subcontinental heritage, there is the additional layer of racism too.

While I am grappling with all the natural worries of any mother, my concerns are additionally overshadowed by this worry. I'm angry that it takes up my emotional space. I'm angry that I have to spend time figuring out how to protect you – not just right now, but also to give you the tools and the resilience to deal with these issues in the future.

My heart breaks a million times knowing that one day very soon I'm going to have to explain to you that there are people in the world who hate you just for being you. Some of them want to make life difficult for you, and – I can hardly bring myself to write the words – some of them might want you dead.

I'm angry because instead of spending time to encourage and enjoy you, I will have to use that precious time in preparing you for a world that may make every effort to block your path and crush your talents and hopes.

I'm angry because instead of being able to nurture you to a point where you can make a full creative contribution to the world, I have to spend time simply proving that we are human, and standing firm until our humanity is recognized and respected.

Even though I spend time thinking these things and working to fight them, I refuse to let this affect how I bring you up, and who you become. The irony is that it is being Muslim which motivates me to bring you up as a shining light. Your job – however you choose to deliver it – is to make the place you live in better. With love and justice.

Sometimes when you wake up in the morning you see me already seated at my desk, writing, like I am right now. When you grow up, I wonder if that is how you will remember me.

What you don't see is that I am writing to challenge the world's hatred of Muslims. What you don't see is that I am working for you to inherit a world where women are treated justly, not unjustly as they are now. What you don't see is my worry that the world is getting harder for a Muslim girl like you. Whatever is within my capability to change this, I will do it. For you. For your little sister. For all the little Muslim girls out there. For *all* the girls. For our collective humanity.

Your father has an important role in this. You see him constantly being my best supporter. You see him valuing and trusting my opinion. You see him encouraging me to be out in the world, owning my voice, unafraid and firm. I hope you are learning from this man right in front of you how good men support women, that men are important in standing shoulder to shoulder with women, giving space to us, giving us strength, showing pride in how we lead the way. My heart bursts with love for him as he does this, because when you grow up you will know that this is what good men do, and I pray that you will not accept anything less in your partner.

What you might not realize till you are older is the value and the rarity of this love, how to find it and to keep it. Forget

Disney movies and happily ever afters. Being a Muslim means I can share with you the verse of the Qur'an where God explains that He has created human beings in pairs, so that we may find love and compassion in each other. Do you see how important compassion is, even in a romantic context?

I wonder whether describing all this to the world is too intimate an approach when trying to change ideas about Muslims like you and me. I've written my story, but should I be sharing yours? I am fierce in protecting you, and yet here I am expressing my deep fears. I could have taken a different route. There are facts about Islamophobia and studies about gender inequality. There are books and reports on rising poverty, and statistics about injustice. I could have been an academic, or a policy-maker, a researcher or a mandarin, even a politician. But if I don't tell the stories that affect my life, then who will? If the choices of Muslim girls and women are restricted directly or indirectly, why shouldn't I be at the front line of the struggle?

When you are old enough, you will stand with me. But I want you to know this one important thing. The struggle today might well be very personal, defending Muslims and Muslim women, because this affects our lives due to the injustice born of hatred. But we are not in this fight simply because it affects us. We are in it because it is *wrong*. It contravenes the principles of being a good human being. And that fight, wherever it is, is a fight that is ours to take on, inspired by the fact that we are Muslim. That's what bringing you up as a Muslim means to me: love and justice. Love for God, and love, compassion and justice for people.

Did I tell you the story of the Prophet Muhammad and how he described what Islam is so simply? 'Love for the Creator, and serving His creation.' And did I tell you what Ali ibn Abi Talib said about how to engage with other people? 'People are of two kinds: either your brothers and sisters in faith, or your equals in humanity.'

I want you to feel surrounded by love. I want you to love being loved, and to love giving love. For love is just a way of finding who you are. Love is the truest expression of you.

As for myself, I'm working towards the same goal, but I don't think I'm living up to it. Maybe I will learn about love from you.

When I was just a little older than you are now, one of my favourite books was *Anne of Green Gables*. The protagonist was feisty and unreserved. Her natural instinct for adventure, intertwined with self-reflection, still appeals to me today. She was herself – and despite this, everyone loved her. It took me a long time to appreciate that actually they loved her *because* of that. At the end of her journey, Anne realizes: 'It's not what the world holds for you, it's what you bring to it.'

My beloved, when you bring love to this world, you will find love in it. But it's important to remember that love is not transactional: you don't find love *in return* for bringing it. When you bring love, that is when you become capable of experiencing it.

My daughter, there is so much to tell you about love, but remember justice and compassion too. Love is only love when it is accompanied by those. As Anne says, the world is only what you bring to it.

Bring love, my beloved daughter, bring love.

Heartbeat

Ayisha Malik

Beenish was fettered by a compulsion to write letters to her dead husbands.

Husband number one, Rahim, had been the long-limbed liar. Compulsively charming in public, and both irritable and irritating in private. Beenish had loved him at first sight – this typically happened to most who met him – so it was almost poetic when one night his heart had given way just as easily.

Dear Rahim,
Today I ate two Weetabix with full fat milk and no sugar. I went to the gym and ran for thirty minutes on the treadmill, which is only fifteen minutes short of what you always said I should be doing when you would laugh and slap my bum. I still find remnants of you all over the house. The other day I came across your nail clippers wedged at the back of the bathroom drawer. I almost didn't throw them away because I'm sure they cost you upwards of thirty pounds . . .

There was a knock on the surgery door. 'Come in,' said Beenish, burying the letter under a pile of paperwork.

The patient approached, draped in a cream headscarf, red lipstick and brazen youth. Beenish felt the twinge of jealousy common to women in their mid-forties when coming across such bold reminders of times past.

'Take a seat,' she said.

The girl, at least that's what she seemed, had sprained her ankle some months ago and it was still giving her problems.

Beenish suggested stronger painkillers and looked at her computer screen. 'I see you're due for a smear test.'

'Oh, I'm not . . .'

A long pause.

'You're not . . .?'

'Sexually active.'

'I'll make a note of that.'

'Only . . .'

The deep red of her lips was distracting. It was practically a spectacle.

'Does that mean *other* stuff too? I mean, I've not had sex or anything. I'm still a virgin. Obviously.'

Obviously!

'But I've *done* stuff. Is that . . . the same thing?'

'You only need a test if you've had penetrative sex.' Beenish wondered about the girl's brand of lipstick. 'Have you?'

The girl shook her head. Beenish considered her hijab. Professionalism in the face of religious pedantry was awfully trying.

'This is entirely confidential and it's better to be honest with me so I can recommend the right course of action.'

'It's just . . . it kind of went in, but only the tip, and you know, nothing happened. Like *inside*.'

'Right. Well, in that case you're fine.'

The girl gave Beenish a shaky smile. Asking her about the lipstick would disturb the doctor–patient balance. Beenish would have to hunt for that crimson shade herself.

*

When her patient had gone, Beenish took the lid off her fountain pen and began a new letter.

Dear Tariq,

There are tulips now blooming in the place where you cracked your neck. Your mum thinks it's a sign from Allah, that the blossoming of life where you died is somehow indicative of how your soul now rests in eternal peace. It's so desperate it makes me feel sorry for her. Still, when I look at the tulips, I remember how you'd often buy me flowers (in lieu of having any kind of real personality). Bless you. But I think, because of the tulips (and you know I'm back into my workout routine), it's time to move on.

Tariq had been her second, and some might say, should have been her *final* husband. As obscure as Rahim had been definitive, Tariq had been a sensible antidote to her previous passion. His death was an accident. A trip, a fall, and death. Poor man. He had ignored his mother's call that morning and she still hadn't forgiven Beenish for it.

One could say that Beenish's experience of marriage so far had been a downward spiral, but her sense of romance remained a burgeoning and boundless entity. She had to get back out there.

Only the tip.

She shook her head as she locked the letters in her drawer and shut down her computer for the day.

*

'I'm looking for a nice shade of red lipstick,' Beenish said to the assistant under the fluorescent lights of Boots.

'You want something with a blue undertone, I think, for your skin colour. Like this?'

It was impossibly glossy.

'Thank you,' said Beenish, pressing it against her finger and then smudging it over her lips.

'That's lovely,' said the assistant. Bright smile, bright teeth.

Beenish looked in the mirror, half her face obscured. The lipstick had aged her at least five years but there was no other option. 'I'll take it. Thank you.'

'Special occasion?'

'Yes. Yes, I think so. I have a date.'

'Ooh, how exciting.'

It *would* be exciting, thought Beenish. A year of mourning had been sufficient. She wasn't twenty-five any more and one had to show expedience when it came to romance. She downloaded a dating app while the assistant scanned the item.

'Good luck,' she said, face impossibly contorted into what Beenish assumed was excitement on her behalf.

There was no mystery to some people.

By the time Beenish had walked home she already had seven matches. Two were prosaic enough in look and profile to be considered inoffensive. One messaged instantly.

Hey, how's your day going?

Being mundane could sometimes be a psychological condition but points had to be given for efficiency, at least.

Her phone rang. She took a deep breath. 'Auntie . . .'

'Sometimes I don't understand,' lamented a voice. 'He was so healthy.'

Beenish bore these phone calls with fortitude. 'I know, Auntie. Me too. I sometimes blame myself . . . my kismet.'

Rahim's mother sobbed. The real tragedy was her wasting any tears over him. Oh sure, Beenish had loved him – vehemently, to the point of sickness even – but it didn't follow that he had deserved it.

'Why don't you come over on the weekend? Spend the day with me?' she suggested.

'I would like that. I would like that very much.'

Beenish would have to forego the gym in favour of allaying these pointless tears – the shackles of marriage alive and well even though her husband was dead. A latent anxiety swelled in her chest as she looked at herself in the mirror, rubbing off the garish lipstick. She threw it in the bin before tapping on her phone.

It's great, thanks. Yours?

The coffee had been arranged within forty-eight hours. A sense of firmness and control sprang to life in Beenish's rightly optimistic heart.

'You look much younger in person. If you don't mind me saying.'

Beenish didn't mind, of course. She was only slightly disconcerted when she realized he was a whole decade younger than her. Attention to detail was something she'd always lacked in relationships.

'Really?'

'What's an attractive, intelligent woman your age doing being single?'

Beenish gripped her coffee mug. Men in their thirties hadn't yet learned the art of being original. Most would get married and settle down without even having to try.

'Never married?' he asked.

She tried to smile. It wasn't her fault that it came across as sad. It was, after all, a sad story. 'Yes, but . . . I'm a widow.'

'God, I'm so sorry. I didn't mean to . . . Sorry.'

She looked down at her coffee. It was never simple. The pain of having lived through death still hurt. The necessity of it. She mourned them both, in her own way. Even Rahim.

'So . . . do you have kids?'

She could see the trepidation in his face, but all that meant was that he must be invested, which in itself was flattering. She shook her head.

'Timing was never right.'

'And now?'

'My womb's clocked out.'

'Ah.' He swallowed hard. 'What happened? To your husband, I mean. Sorry, that's a very personal question. You don't have to –'

'Thank you.'

Eventually she would have to tell him about both of them, but judging the right moment was crucial. There was the predictable lull in conversation – a need to segue from widowhood into something less demoralizing.

'Great weather we're having,' he said. 'Sorry, that was . . .'

'Not the smoothest.' She smiled to show she was being playful. One had to demonstrate these things. There was too much room for error in dating.

He laughed. A small one. Rather charming, in fact, this bashfulness. He looked at her, inquisitive, as if trying to decipher her, and Beenish felt a sense of power that she knew was the stepping stone to love.

'I'll give you another go,' she said.

'The pressure.'

'Think of this as a practice run,' she said.

'Have you been back in the dating game long?'

'No. This is *my* practice run.' She took a sip of her coffee, looking him in the eye.

He laughed again. Another inquisitive look. This was going well.

'You're different, aren't you?' he said.

'Not at all. I am quite regular.'

As they left the coffee shop on the South Bank by the Thames, the inky sky tinted with streaks of orange and sprinkled with stars, he said, 'Next time, let's get dinner and we can put this practice run to the test.'

And her heart fluttered. Oh, how it fluttered.

Rahim's mum was made up entirely of sighs and sobs. She sat on Beenish's sofa, taking up more space than her diminutive frame intended.

'I can't stay too long.' She shifted on the velvet sofa that had foam-wrapped feathers and down padding. 'Your uncle needs me.'

'Ah, yes, Uncle.'

'Men, beta. They can't live without us. In the end.'

'I don't suppose they can.'

'It is a sign of having been a good wife.'

Beenish's lips twitched. Her natural romanticism had not translated into natural servitude and this had been a quandary in both marriages. Her phone pinged.

Dinner next Friday?

Rahim's mum watched her closely. Beenish was smiling, which didn't go well with her mother-in-law's tears. Although was 'mother-in-law' now technically correct?

'Who is it?' she asked with contrived nonchalance.

'A friend,' Beenish answered.

'Hmm.'

Beenish disguised the thudding of her heart with a flickering smile.

'Aleesha?' asked her mother-in-law.

What was the name for a dead husband's mother?

'No, Tahseen.'

Beenish hadn't heard from Tahseen in months. Husbands weren't the only things she was capable of losing.

'Her children must be so grown-up now?'

'The eldest is in her first year of uni.'

'Mashallah.' Her mother-in-law sighed. 'If only you'd had a child. Your parents gone so soon and no siblings either. You wouldn't be alone.'

Beenish's parents had died in a car accident when she was eighteen. Being an only child, she'd seldom faced anything other than adoration and believed, by virtue of experience, that this was how it would always be. She was in for a shock. When it came to negotiating Rahim's changeable charm, this had been outside the ambit of her emotional intelligence.

So, naturally, before her husbands, and subsequent to each one, there'd been plenty of emphasis on Beenish being alone. Attempts at alleviating her aloneness hadn't been quite so emphatic.

'And I'd have a grandchild to remember him by,' her mother-in-law grieved.

'Let me just check on the chicken.' Beenish took her phone with her into the kitchen. It pinged.

Friday sounds good. Let's make it 8 p.m. I've been wanting to try Benito's in Covent Garden if that's OK?

Italian was perhaps a bit heavy. Having pasta or pizza at eight o'clock in the evening wasn't a great idea if she wanted to keep her figure. But it was too late now. He couldn't think her indecisive.

'We have to keep his memory alive,' Beenish replied, returning to the living room. 'And pray for him.' Which Beenish did, every day, without fail. She believed in both retribution and forgiveness.

'You must think of yourself now too,' said her mother-in-law.

'I do.'

'Are you . . .' Her mother-in-law seemed to look anywhere but at Beenish.

'Am I . . .?'

'You understand how two husbands . . . like that. Just gone. People talk.'

'What do they say?'

Her mother-in-law fidgeted. Beenish could sense her father-in-law's hand in this.

'I have bad luck,' Beenish said eventually. She couldn't blame people for talking. It certainly was a bad run. 'I knew it when Amma and Baba died.' Something snagged in Beenish's throat.

'Allah's will,' replied her mother-in-law. 'But look at you . . . a doctor, mashallah. Your parents would have been so proud. And you wear makeup and nice clothes and still look so young. Oh, you know I don't mind these things, but people . . .'

'Yes. People. What do you say to them?'

'Me?'

'Yes. What do you tell them?'

It was the kind of pause that had all the makings of a rupture.

'Well, I don't say anything.'

Beenish understood. She was, after all, a woman of the world. 'I think the roast is done.'

*

Rahim,
You should know that I've not been ruined by your sociopathic tendencies. I still trust. You would call it

stupidity, but I call it optimism. You did not spoil men for me. You lost in more ways than one.

*

The crowd heaved in waves through the door of Benito's, the place filled with cotton dresses, loosened ties, and the undercurrent of summer's possibilities. Beenish felt the damp under her armpits that had always repelled Rahim. It was, to his mind, unseemly for a woman to sweat. Or take a piss or a shit. (Beenish now exhibited her freedom by using the toilet with the door open.)

'This place is packed,' Asif said.

The words 'The One' had always suggested uniqueness to Beenish; unlike any other; a rarity, the shock of which would snake its way into one's psyche and veins. Love was a drug far more powerful than the ones she prescribed for her patients. And the lack of it made one feel one a mixture of despondence and panic.

'That's a good sign,' she replied.

'Let's hope so,' he said pointedly.

Their laughter was indistinguishable from anyone else's. Asif hadn't realized that what he thought was a connection simply attested to Beenish's experience in relationships.

She leaned forward, casting furtive glances around them. 'Everyone thinks they're so *individual*, don't they?'

'Aren't we?'

'How old are you really?'

'Old enough.'

'I'm not so sure.' She squinted at him, twirled the glass of sparkling water in her hand. He glanced at the first few buttons of her shirt, which were undone. 'And how would your parents feel about you dating an older woman?' she added.

'Like I said, I'm old enough.'

*

Tariq,

I think you'd like Asif. But I still have guilt. Not for Rahim, of course, but you deserved better. Then again, in some ways I did too. I'd like to fall in love again. You get that – we had that in common, our hopefulness. Guess it goes to show that having things in common can't save a marriage. Or a life.

*

Over the following months, Beenish's days flitted between flirtation and work. She had tried on another red lipstick she found at a Space NK and was striding home, watching for glances of admiration from passing strangers, when her eyes fell on a familiar face.

'Auntie,' began Beenish.

Tariq's mum was an elongated figure of disapproval. She gave Beenish the once-over. Her daughter-in-law's lipstick, demeanour and the confidence which the knowledge of being desired brings out in a person were all there for Tariq's mother to judge.

'How are you?' Beenish asked.

'I see *you're* doing well.'

And why shouldn't she be? Was she to grieve for ever? Even in Islam women only had to mourn for three months before considering marriage again. Alas, you could free yourself of religion, but never of people.

'Thank you.'

Love – or its ilk – emboldened people and Tariq's mum objected to boldness of any kind. Especially when it came from a woman.

'You've forgotten my son very quickly.'

Beenish gave a small smile. 'He would've hated for me to dwell.' Which was true.

Being desired could also make people insolent. Vocal. Fearless. Though Beenish had feared very little, other than the idea of never being loved. It was a common weakness, at least.

'You're mistaken,' his mum said. 'He would've hated for you to think otherwise. That was the kind of man my son was.'

Before Beenish could reply, Tariq's mum added, 'Allah knows best,' as she walked away.

Even religion could be reduced to passive aggression.

*

Rahim's mother's calls became incessant. Who'd have thought that her other mother-in-law could possess a woman's intuition? Beenish ignored her, but with each call the woman's urgency for commitment increased. She left voicemails: *Beta, if you have a few minutes, I need to talk to you about something important.*

Subtlety and privacy had never quite made it into the Pakistani consciousness. Beenish was used to it but, with age, habits were set, and at the same time longstanding ways were tolerated less.

She was walking through St James's Park with Asif, enjoying the autumn sunshine, when her phone rang. It was Rahim's mum again.

'Salaam alaykum, Auntie.' The conversation had hardly begun and Beenish was already feeling impatient. It was one thing to be tied down to husbands, but to be tied down to their mums after those husbands' deaths was quite another frustration.

'Sorry I haven't called sooner,' she said. 'Work's been busy.'

'I hear you ran into Tariq's ammi.'

'Yes.'

'She had things to say.'

'That doesn't surprise me.'

'Tell me . . . you won't lie to me, will you?'

Beenish had to take a deep breath. 'Of course not.'

'Do you plan to get married again?' There was a quiver in her voice. Other people's emotions could be exhausting.

'It's not . . . I don't know.'

'Tariq's mum is not . . . well, she's not behaving very Islamically. She is saying things . . . things that suggest our sons' deaths – '

'What about the deaths?'

'That they were *suspicious*.'

Beenish felt her heartbeat quicken. 'I see.'

'She's found out – and I don't mind, I understand these things – but she's found out about the man you are seeing.'

Fucking aunties. No one gets in the way of romantic love more than them. Even without parents or siblings, everything Beenish did seemed to be under the ownership of someone else. It was infantilizing.

'And?'

'Does *he* know? About both of them? You are like my own daughter. I want you to be happy.'

'Yes, he knows. Of course, he knows.'

Beenish ended the call to tell her boyfriend that she had not one, but two dead husbands. Tariq's death was somehow more alarming to Asif than Rahim's.

'He just fell?'

'Yes.'

They sat on a bench to drink their coffees. London was a palette of grey concrete and red and orange leaves, scattered in their path. So began their first serious argument. Beenish knew that even though it was important to understand the patchwork of emotions that constituted how a partner might love you, it was just as important to understand how they might argue with you: one so often defined the other. There were accusations of secrecy, of not letting him in, which Beenish denied so passionately that even she herself believed it.

'I find it hard, you see,' she said. 'To talk about things.'

His voice softened. 'You should be able to tell me anything. And something like this – how could I not know after three months of dating you? What else haven't you told me?'

'Nothing.' She leaned her head against his chest, gently kissed the line of his jaw and took a deep breath. 'It's just, don't you see?' She looked up at him. 'My husbands, my parents . . . Life for me is death.' She felt tears prickle her eyes.

Asif put his arm around her. 'It's the first time I've seen you like this,' he said.

Beenish tried to even her breathing. 'Sorry, I . . .'

'No, don't be sorry. You're just so strong – after all you've been through. I don't think I've met anyone like you before.'

She was perhaps unique enough for the both of them. 'You can't get out much.'

'I've been out *a lot.*'

Beenish could feel the damp of the bench.

'I told my parents about you,' he added.

'Oh. And?'

He looked at the ground, a small smile. 'It could've been worse.'

'I see.'

'But it doesn't matter. They'll come round in the end.'

'How can you be sure?'

'I'm their only son.'

A mild panic fluttered in Beenish's otherwise calm chest. 'Of course.'

He held on to her, tightened his grip. Beenish allowed him to feel needed just as much as she enjoyed the feeling of needing him. It was the mathematics of love, and certain calculations reaped more rewards than others.

*

Beenish went into Selfridges and approached a sales assistant made up of every artificiality you could think of, from painted toenails to fake eyelashes and micro-bladed brows. She was the definition of generic beauty.

'Do you need help?' Her lips barely moved. From afar she had looked in her twenties. Up close she looked almost forty – foundation creasing in the faint wrinkles around her eyes and mouth.

'I'm getting married.'

'Oh, congratulations,' she said, with a smile that suggested she'd heard this often enough.

'I'm looking for a red lipstick. It's hard, with my skin tone.'

'Hmm.' The generic beauty looked at her thoughtfully. She went and brought back several lipsticks with mini brushes, a spray, and a box of tissues. It took several tries before Beenish liked what she saw in the mirror.

'This one isn't too bad,' she murmured.

'No,' replied the assistant, her eyes flickering around the fluorescently lit floor before settling on Beenish and giving her another smile. 'Not at all. I'd say it's almost perfect.'

'Almost,' said Beenish.

'I mean, it *is* perfect. Just look.' She held up the mirror so Beenish could see her full face. It was possibly the best she was going to find. Her phone buzzed.

What do you think of this tie?

The attached picture was of Asif wearing a deep red tie and nothing else. She felt something stir inside her and put her phone away.

'I think this lipstick really suits you.'

'It'll be for my wedding day itself.'

'Perfect,' the assistant repeated.

It wasn't perfect, but Beenish was adult enough to know that things hardly ever were.

'It'll do,' she said to the assistant. 'For now.'

In the Uber on the way home, she got out her notepad.

Dear Rahim and Tariq,
He's so different from both of you. And you were so
different from one another. It'd be silly to fall for the
same sort of man over and over again. This time, things
will be different. I am sure of it.

It was satisfying. Closure. She took out her Chanel mirror and smiled at herself, the matte red seeping into the tiny cracks in her lips. Her phone beeped in her handbag.

I can't wait to spend the rest of my life with you.

Her smile faltered. She recalled the giving way of Rahim's heart, the crack of Tariq's neck. The necessity of both. Just as with them, only time would tell how long the rest of any life might be.

Biographical Notes

Nazneen Ahmed lives in Southampton. She writes fiction for children, creative nonfiction, and poetry for adults. Her writing is often inspired by the theme of migration, which is the topic of her work as a researcher and historian in the Geography Department at University College London. She was selected for the 2016–17 round of Penguin Random House's WriteNow mentorship scheme for under-represented writers for her historical fantasy novel in progress, which is aimed at readers aged eleven upwards. From June 2016 to July 2017 Nazneen was the SO: Write UK Southampton Libraries' Writer in Residence. She is represented by Louise Lamont at LBA Books.

*

Sufiya Ahmed is the author of the 'Zahra at the Khadija Academy' series and the Young Adult bestseller *Secrets of the Henna Girl* (Puffin, 2012). Sufiya was born in India and arrived in the UK as a baby. She lived in Bolton, Lancashire, before moving to London where she still lives. Sufiya has worked in advertising and in the House of Commons, but is now a full-time author. In 2010 she set up the BIBI Foundation, a non-profit organization which arranges visits to the Houses of Parliament for diverse and underprivileged schoolchildren.

*

Sunah Ahmed was born and brought up in Glasgow, Scotland. She studied Journalism and Creative Writing with English Literature at Strathclyde University before pursuing a postgraduate degree in English teaching. Alongside her education work she writes poetry and short stories, which are often inspired by her surroundings and her Scottish-Pakistani culture. Sunah enjoys reading a range of texts and her love for literature was originally sparked by American-Dominican writer Junot Díaz.

*

Nafhesa Ali is a sociologist and was the lead postdoctoral researcher for the Storying Relationships project at the University of Sheffield. Nafhesa is a third-generation British Muslim whose family have been settled in West Yorkshire since the 1960s. This heritage has provided a strong foundation for her research interests in gender, ageing, the life course and creative methods. Nafhesa's publications include the co-authored forthcoming Zed book *Storying Relationships: Young British Muslims Speak and Write About Sex and Love* (2020), 'Halal Dating: Changing Relationship Attitudes and Experiences

Among Young British Muslims' in *Sexualities* (2019), and 'Understanding Generation Through the Lens of Ethnic and Cultural Diversity' in *Families, Relationships and Societies* (2014).

*

Claire Chambers teaches postcolonial literature, and Zumba on the side. Her fascination with Muslim South Asia was ignited by a teenage year spent in Peshawar in the 1990s. The interest continues to be fuelled by visits to the subcontinent and engagement work with Muslim communities in Britain. Claire is a Senior Lecturer in Global Literature at the University of York and has worked as Editor-in-Chief of the *Journal of Commonwealth Literature* for a decade. She has edited three collections and is the author of four books, including most recently *Rivers of Ink: Selected Essays* (2018) and *Making Sense of Contemporary British Muslim Novels* (2019). She also writes a regular column for the Pakistani national newspaper *Dawn*.

*

Afshan D'souza-Lodhi is the Editor-in-Chief of the Common Sense Network, an online news resource. She is an award-winning writer of plays and poetry, and was recently commissioned to write and direct a short film for Channel 4. She has completed residencies at the Royal Exchange Theatre and Manchester Literature Festival, and has worked with Eclipse Theatre, the Tamasha Theatre Company and Paul Burston's Polari. Afshan has edited several anthologies, as well as publishing an essay in a high-profile collection by Muslim women *It's Not About the Burqa* (2019). In addition to her own writing, Afshan is keen to develop other younger and emerging artists, and sits on the boards of Manchester Literature Festival and Brighter Sound.

*

Roopa Farooki is the author of six critically acclaimed novels: *The Good Children*, *The Flying Man*, *Half Life*, *The Way Things Look to Me*, *Corner Shop* and *Bitter Sweets*, published by Headline and Macmillan. She has been shortlisted for the Orange Award for New Writers and the Muslim Writers' Awards, and has also been longlisted for the Women's Prize (twice), the DSC South Asian Literature Prize and the Impac Dublin Literary Award. Her books have been published internationally in thirteen countries across Europe, and in the US. She was awarded an Arts Council Literature award, and the John C. Laurence award from the Authors' Foundation for writing which improves understanding between races. Roopa lectures on the Creative Writing Masters at the University of Oxford and recently completed her degree in Medicine at St George's, University of London. Following her 2016 shortlisting for the Commonword Prize for Children's Fiction, Roopa is currently working on diverse fiction for young people.

*

Noren Haq is a Muslim mother of three who home educates her children using the unschooling method. She has an MA in English Literature and a PGDE in secondary education.

Biographical Notes

Noren spent several happy years as an English teacher and ran an extracurricular creative writing club for pupils aspiring to become authors. She has written a number of short stories, three children's picture books and a play; the latter was penned while participating in the Storying Relationships creative writing workshops held at Glasgow Women's Library. Noren loves all things fusion and is currently researching her novel, a cross-cultural Regency murder mystery.

*

Zarina Harriri is a Scottish-Pakistani Muslim woman. She started writing poetry at the age of eight and has always found it easier to express her emotions and feelings on paper than in conversation. During university she regularly blogged to condense her thoughts and ramblings into posts. She mostly kept her blog posts private but sometimes showed them to close friends. Zarina only recently began writing fiction when she realized her mind frequently ran away with her. She felt that sharing her stories and ideas would not only bring out everyday issues which exist amongst Muslim women but also make people laugh. She writes to understand others and to help others understand her. Although each of her characters has their own personality, she frequently projects traits of her own onto her literary creations.

*

Sarvat Hasin was born in London and grew up in Karachi. She studied Politics and International Relations at Royal Holloway and then took a Masters in Creative Writing at the University of Oxford. Her first novel, *This Wide Night*, was published by Penguin India and longlisted for the DSC Prize for South Asian Literature. Her second book, *You Can't Go Home Again*, was published in 2018 and was featured in the end of year lists in *Vogue India* and *The Hindu*. She won the Moth Writers Retreat Bursary in 2018. Her essays and poetry have appeared in publications such as *On Anxiety*, *The Mays Anthology*, *English PEN* and *Harper's Bazaar*.

*

Sairish Hussain was born and brought up in Bradford, West Yorkshire. She studied English Language and Literature at the University of Huddersfield and progressed to an MA in Creative Writing where she began working on her first novel. Sairish recently completed her PhD successfully after being awarded Huddersfield University's Vice-Chancellor's Scholarship. Her novel, *The Family Tree*, was published by HQ (HarperCollins) in 2020.

*

Inayah Jamil is a twenty-year-old Scottish-Pakistani Muslim woman who hopes to bring back the love of God into the hearts of humanity. She also wants to influence positive change by inspiring others through her creative writing voice. Inayah has been writing ever since her early years at school, sparked by her own personal life challenges.

Biographical Notes

Shelina Janmohamed is the bestselling author of *Love in a Headscarf*, a humorous memoir about growing up as a British Muslim woman. Her book, *Generation M:Young Muslims Changing the World*, explores a rising group of global Muslims who believe that faith and modernity go hand in hand. A recognized global expert on cultural and religious trends, particularly around young Muslims and Muslim women, she writes for the *Telegraph*, the *Guardian*, the *National* and the BBC, amongst others. She was named one of the UK's 100 most powerful Muslim women. Shelina lives in London with her husband and two daughters. You can follow her @loveinheadscarf.

*

Sabyn Javeri is the author of the political novel *Nobody Killed Her* (2017) and *Hijabistan* (2019), a collection of short stories about life beyond the veil. Her fiction focuses on issues of identity and gender politics, and has been published in the *London Magazine*, the *South Asian Review*, *Bengal Lights*, *Wasafiri* and *Sugar Mule* amongst others, as well as in anthologies published by HarperCollins, Oxford University Press and the Feminist Press. She has won the *Oxonian Review* Short Story Award and was shortlisted for the Leaf Prize and the Tibor Jones South Asia Prize. Sabyn has edited two volumes of the *Arzu Anthology of Student Voices* (Vol. 1: 2018, Vol. 2: 2019) – a first of its kind creative writing initiative in higher education in Pakistan. Sabyn is a graduate of the University of Oxford and has a PhD from Leicester University. She lives between the UK and Pakistan and is an assistant professor in Literature and

Creative Writing at Habib University, Karachi and New York University Abu Dhabi.

*

Ayisha Malik is a writer and editor, living in south London. She holds a BA in English Literature and a First-Class MA in Creative Writing. Her novels include *Sofia Khan is Not Obliged* (2015), *The Other Half of Happiness* (2017) and *This Green and Pleasant Land* (2019); she also contributed to the anthology *A Change is Gonna Come* (2017). Ayisha was a WH Smith Fresh Talent Pick, shortlisted for the Asian Women of Achievement Award and for *Marie Claire*'s Future Shapers Awards. She is also the ghost-writer for *The Great British Bake Off* winner, Nadiya Hussain.

*

Mariam Naeem is a Scottish-Pakistani woman who fell in love with creative writing at a young age and has been writing ever since. She has published poetry and has a blog on Vocal Media about health that is dedicated to spreading positivity and motivation. Mariam comes from a single-parent Muslim family. Her mother was widowed when Mariam was seven, and since then Mariam has had to deal with problems that she considers outside the norm for a young Muslim woman, such as relatives' addictions and assuming responsibility for siblings. Mariam offers an unusual but still important viewpoint about relationships, as she is neither religious nor much involved with

British-Pakistani culture. She wants to discuss sides of Muslim life that many prefer not to speak about: so-called 'shame', relationships outside marriage, divorce, and independent women.

*

Richard Phillips is Professor of Human Geography at the University of Sheffield. He is a specialist in creative and arts-led research methodologies, which he practises in his own work and encourages students to try in the field trips he leads in cities including Liverpool, Berlin, Vancouver and New York. Richard was the lead researcher in Storying Relationships, the project behind this book, on which he worked with Claire Chambers and Nafhesa Ali. His publications include *Sex, Politics and Empire* (1996), *Mapping Men and Empire: A Geography of Adventure* (1997), *Muslim Spaces of Hope* (2008), *Fieldwork for Human Geography* (2012) and *Georges Perec's Geographies* (2019).

*

Shaista Sadick is an author of short stories, an amateur comedian, a sometimes calligrapher, and a global mutt. She has spent time in Karachi, Lahore, London and Singapore, and now lives in Newcastle. Shaista has two dogs and two cats, one husband and three kids. With whatever time she has left, she is a video-game scriptwriter. This job isn't nearly as glamorous as it sounds, but it pays the bills and means she's slaughtered many a demon king in her time.

Biographical Notes

Bina Shah is a Karachi-based author of five novels and two collections of short stories. Her novels include the critically acclaimed *A Season for Martyrs* (2014) and the feminist dystopian novel *Before She Sleeps* (2018). She has been a regular contributor to the *New York Times*, *Al Jazeera* and the *Huffington Post*, and is a frequent guest on the BBC. Bina is a graduate of Wellesley College and the Harvard Graduate School of Education, and is an Honorary Fellow in Writing at the University of Iowa. She is currently the president of the Alliance Française de Karachi and writes on issues of women's rights and female empowerment in Pakistan and across Muslim countries.

Acknowledgements

Our gratitude goes to all of the authors in *A Match Made in Heaven*, both new and established. We were blown away by the experienced writers' ready agreement to contribute to the anthology, and by the humour, thoughtfulness and originality of their stories.

Workshops for our emerging writers were led by the playwright Sara Shaarawi, novelist Safina Mazhar, bloggers Talat Yaqoob and Faiza Yousaf, by the artist Stacy Bias and writers Afshan D'souza-Lodhi, Mohammed Barber, Atta Yaqub and John Siddique. To them we give our heartfelt thanks.

We would also like to acknowledge the many others who attended workshops, encouraging each other with feedback, camaraderie and constructive criticism. Too numerous to mention, they form a movement in which young British Muslims are finding their writerly voices.

We thank all those who convened and hosted the workshops, edited the written work and provided platforms for the collection to be published. We extend particular gratitude

Acknowledgements

to Syma Ahmed, the Women's Project Development Worker at the Glasgow Women's Library (GWL). This is a library we have come to love and admire, and which has itself been a key partner in this project. Others who supported these workshops and young writers, and who we regard as friends of the project, include Kamal Kaan, Syima Aslam (Bradford Literature Festival) and Sheraz Mohammed (Hemer Youth Group, Rochdale).

Some of the stories printed in this book and others told within the broader project have also been brought to life on the stage and through the medium of film. For this work we wish to acknowledge Edinburgh's Stellar Quines Theatre Company, and filmmakers Cathy Giles and Ben Giles (https://www.matobo.co.uk/). Short films about the project and readings of a selection of stories by authors in this book, and others too, can be viewed online at www.sheffield.ac.uk/storyingrelationships).

The last stage in this process has been made rigorous and enjoyable by the dedication of HopeRoad. We are especially grateful to the visionary publisher Rosemarie Hudson, and to our meticulous copy editor Joan Deitch. HopeRoad have been a great support throughout our publication process and are committed to more honest and authentic routes for audiences to engage with Muslim communities and stories.

This project, entitled Storying Relationships, which ran from 2016 to 2019, was funded through a grant from the Arts and Humanities Research Council (AHRC).

Finally, we would like to acknowledge you, the reader of this book, for making time for these stories of love and desire. Doing so, you become part of a bigger story which confounds

Acknowledgements

expectations about what it means to be young, female and Muslim, and widens perceptions of who can be a writer. You, dear reader, are part of something creative, challenging, playful and exciting.

Claire Chambers, Nafhesa Ali, and Richard Phillips
https://www.sheffield.ac.uk/storyingrelationships